A BETRAYAL AT EASTWICK

L. C. WARMAN

greenleaf &
plympton

Address:
Greenleaf & Plympton
P.O. Box 36621
18640 Mack Ave.
Grosse Pointe Farms, MI 48236-9998

Greenleaf & Plympton is a publisher of gothic books, both classic and modern. To see our full catalog, visit www.greenleafandplympton.com.

Cover art: Caroline Teagle Johnson

Proofreading: Alexandra Ott

Library of Congress Control Number: 2019944387

ISBN (e-book) 978-1-950103-18-8

ISBN (print) 978-1-950103-19-5

A BETRAYAL AT EASTWICK

CHAPTER 1

aniel Becker, known to the world as "Becks," always *knew* it could happen to him. But he had been lucky in life, lucky enough to get a full ride to college on a football scholarship, lucky enough to be a first-draft pick in the NFL, lucky enough to meet and marry the love of his life before he had turned twenty-three.

Except now, his luck had changed.

And that *thing* that he didn't want to speak of, didn't want even to think about, was happening to him.

Undeniable. That was the word Whitney had used, fear in her eyes, a question in her voice. Still not wanting to believe the worst.

"Ready, sweetheart?"

Becks started. Whitney stood behind him, dark hair drawn back into a wispy low bun, cocktail dress glimmering as the sequins picked up the low lamplight of their four-bedroom house. She looked exactly as she did that night, ten years before, when he had met her at a college fraternity party, except then she had been shy and overwhelmed, and now she looked sad and worried. He wanted to reach out and sweep the anxious lines from her forehead. He wanted to tell her that his head hurt, without *that thing* slithering between them.

"I'm ready," Becks said brightly, and smiled. The movement sent a jolt of pain to the back of his skull, but he took care not to show it.

"The car's outside." She hesitated. "You're *sure*, Daniel? You seem a little tired."

"I'm not, Whit. You always think that." He reached out and squeezed her hand, and she squeezed it back with a sigh.

"I suppose Evan wouldn't forgive us if we skipped," she muttered, leading the way out into the cool March night.

"Oh, never."

"Have you called him?"

"Texted. He wants to give a speech later in the night, when everyone's arrived."

"I hope he doesn't expect you to say something."

That hurt, but he let it slide, seeing the quick anxiety in Whitney's face. "No, honey," he said. "Evan's the brains behind the organization. I'm just there to stand around and look pretty."

He tried to make the words sound light, but his head still hurt, and they came out resentful and petulant. He hated that voice. It was one he heard more and more often. Self-pity, the vice above all others that he wished to avoid.

"You're the brains, and the money, and the face," Whitney said, squeezing his hand as they climbed into the black SUV that was to take them to the party. "Evan couldn't do any of this without you—don't forget that."

"And you think it's a good idea?"

"You keep asking me that, Daniel. I told you, I think it's a good idea because *you* do. Evan's your oldest friend. He's been working on the business for years. With your funding, and connections—well, I don't pretend to understand it, but certainly, yes, I think it's as good an idea as any."

"A better idea than going to business school," Becks said.

Whitney shot him a look of warning and passed him a water bottle from the SUV's center console. Their driver, a thin man with a wispy gray mustache, was professional enough to read in their manners that he should remain silent. Becks studied him for a few moments, wondering if he would trade places with him, wondering if the man's mind, old and softening as it might be, was stronger than his own. Faster. Cleverer.

The party was at the Eastwick mansion, or rather, the place formerly known as the Eastwick mansion—it had been sold in February, by John Eastwick Sr.'s widow and son, in a fit of caprice that still left tongues wagging. There were rumors that something had happened in the mansion, months ago, but those had been vague and unsettled, and the consensus was now that the wife was too distraught to try to take care of the sprawling family heirloom, and was going to pack herself up and move to a condo in downtown St. Clair, or, horror of all horrors, out to the city itself, amidst the skyscrapers and bustle and away from the sleepy, opulent, lakeside wonders of the town.

Becks didn't much care where the party was being held—Evan had rented the mansion, had organized the party, had planned the catering and the sound system and all the other million little details. And Evan had joked with Becks that it was all because he loved pomp and grandeur, because he couldn't very well start a new business venture with Becks, his friend of fifteen years (since they were both pimply high school freshmen, as Evan liked to say), without making a big fuss about it. "I love attention," Evan would say, sighing. "You know me."

Except Evan wasn't like that at all. Evan was trying to help him, too, in his own way. To take his mind off of things, though Evan would never be so foolish as to put it like that. To bring Becks out into society again, to force him to mingle and interact with people who, if they had followed sports news at all in the past few months, knew all about Becks' ignominious and sudden retirement.

"Shoot," Whitney said, checking her purse. She clucked and dug through the layers of keys and receipts and lipglosses. "I think I forgot my phone."

"It's fine."

He said it calmly—he thought he said it calmly—but Whitney tensed, eyes darting up to him. "Sorry," she said quickly. "Could you call it? Please? Sorry, Daniel."

"You don't have to apologize," he said, and Whitney winced again, gaze shifting to the driver, who was still pretending to ignore them. Becks cleared his throat. He could never sound right these days. Everything that he said came out angry, hostile. He would ask about the weather and Whitney would spook, telling him to change his tone. Change his tone? Half the time he didn't even realize it had changed.

He called her phone. Seconds later, a peppy jingle started.

"Oh, here it is," Whitney said, relieved. She pulled it from the seat, where it had wedged beneath her, and waved it at him.

Daniel noticed, as she settled back in, that she had scooted as far away from him as possible.

CHAPTER 2

*E*van Miller ran a hand through his curly hair, keeping one eye on the entrance. He checked his watch again, foot tapping as he leaned up against the wall dividing the banquet hall from the atrium, both places already swelling with people.

Late. Of course Becks would be late. Whitney probably wasn't helping—she babied him, fussed over him. A man couldn't live with that kind of mothering; it made him into a blathering idiot. A second thought followed that, and Evan shuddered.

It's under control, he reminded himself. The party was just a formality, a fun diversion that he and Whitney had agreed would be good for Becks and for everyone. It was one of the few things they had agreed upon the past few months, but then, with all the planning, who wouldn't be stressed?

Becker & Miller Associates was to be opened at the end of the week, taking up a small office in downtown St. Clair, not far from the high school where Evan and Becks had met. Becks had been large even then: a big, blond bear with a ready smile and hands the size of dinner plates, who was too shy to do well with girls and too driven to get into too much trouble.

Becks' parents weren't wealthy and weren't poor—they lived outside of St. Clair, but the St. Clair football coach had wanted Becks so badly that he had pulled some strings, dangling the much-better public school and his connections to college coaches in front of Becks' parents, so that on that first day freshman year, when Becks thundered through the glass doors, half the school already knew his name.

Evan had homeroom with him and moved right in. "We're going to be friends," he told Becks.

The shy fourteen-year-old had blushed. "Okay," he said. "Why's that?"

"Because you'll make it infinitely easier for me to walk down the hall," Evan had said. "Right now, it's a nightmare."

Becks had laughed, and their friendship took off. Oh, they had their rough patches, over the years. Evan had gone to a different college, so they had spent some time apart, promising to catch up and never following through. Then, when Becks had been drafted to the Gryphons, Evan had reached back out, suggesting drinks, since he too had moved back to work at the city's largest accounting firm. Once, when Evan was twenty-two, he had raged at Becks for not taking him to a football and cheerleader party because Becks had a fiancée (Whitney, then and always). Another time, when Becks was twenty-five or twenty-six, Becks had told Evan, quite seriously, that he was worried about Evan's "influence" on his lifestyle— a declaration that Evan first thought came from Whitney, and only later realized came from Becks' parents...though given subsequent events, he had chosen not to touch *that* with a ten-foot pole.

The long and the short of it was that they had been together for most of their adult lives. And after Becks' fallout with his family, Evan was now the longest relationship he had. Evan felt a burst of something like pity at this, and smoothed it over. Becks wouldn't want that.

The party would get Becks out of the house, at least, and

also generate some publicity. Some *good* publicity. And, as Evan had explained to Whitney and Becks over and over, these types of ventures didn't go anywhere without publicity.

"Where's the man of the night?"

The voice shook Evan out of his reverie, and he turned to find Aaron Williamson striding towards him. They shook hands, Evan's fingers swallowed in Aaron's, and then Evan said, "Should be here any minute. Whitney's coming, too."

"Ah, lovely," Aaron said. "A wife. That's what I need. You got one?"

Evan found the statement odd, but he wouldn't pretend to understand some of Becks' football friends. Aaron Williamson was a tight end with the Gryphons. He and Sam O'Nally, the other football player there that night, were the only ones who would agree to be seen in public with Becks at this point. Aaron Williamson because he got along with everyone, Sam O'Nally because he got along with no one—no one, that is, except for Becks.

"Eh?" Aaron said, nudging him. But Aaron's eyes were circling the party, scanning for—well, at first Evan thought he was scanning for women, any women, but it seemed he was looking for someone in particular.

"A wife?" Evan said. "No, I don't have one."

"A girlfriend?"

"No." He thought of Rhiannon, who had dumped a bag of almond flour onto his new shag carpet when he had told her that he didn't want anything serious. *You could have said that a little earlier,* she had snarled, which struck him as nonsensical. Almost as nonsensical as dumping flour onto a carpet.

"Smart man," Aaron said. "They're more trouble than they're worth. Say, speaking of, you've seen Eliza?"

"Who?"

"Eliza Vorne. I came with her. Well, not came with her, exactly. I mean…never mind." Aaron grinned sheepishly. "You let me know if you see her, okay?"

7

"Sure." One of Whitney's friends, Evan remembered.

"Just look for the finest woman in the room. I can say that because you don't have a wife," Aaron said, winking before he disappeared into the crowd. Evan sighed and downed his champagne. He felt a heavy sense of foreboding. *It's not too late to back out,* a voice whispered in his ear, and he shoved it back down. This is what he had dreamed about for years, after all. What they had dreamed about.

Evan felt mildly sick.

$\mathcal{E}$liza took a flute of champagne from a waiter's passing tray and then did her best to angle her body away from Aaron. The benefit of dating (or having dated) a football player was that it was so easy to spot them—in a crowd, at a bar, in the park. She could easily find Aaron or avoid him, as her desires dictated.

Tonight, it was avoid. Whitney had invited her, and given all that the poor woman was going through, Eliza felt duty-bound to accept. Still, zipped into her tight, sequined green dress, hair stiff with spray and shoes throbbing in designer heels, Eliza couldn't help but think about how much better it would all be if she were wrapped in a blanket at this exact moment, watching a crime television show with a glass of red wine.

She sighed. She did, of course, still have business to attend to tonight.

As if that weren't enough, there was the putrid little fact that Gina Tiller had made her way to the party. The woman had been grinning at her as Eliza entered the Eastwick place, trying to hold eye contact long enough to justify coming over. As if Eliza would have ever given her the time of day, even *before*. Unlike Evan Miller, Eliza was not impressed by power and wealth—she had come from enough of it. Unlike Evan Miller, she would not become a sycophant to some spoiled princess whose father owned the Gryphons, and *especially* not if that spoiled princess was also a—

Well.

Eliza tapped her foot, pretending to survey the table of appetizers behind her. Shrimp cocktails, bruschetta, candied nuts, prosciutto. She would just stay long enough for Whitney to come and see her. And then she'd make her excuses—*so sorry, early morning, test shoot for a special later this week*. Whitney would understand; they had met in college, in a broadcast communications course, and though Whitney went on to become a teacher and then (even more work) the wife of a professional football player, Eliza had worked her way up from local television stations to a syndicated program across the tri-state area—with a potential promotion to New York on the horizon. Aaron had hated the idea, which made Eliza love it all the more.

"I've been looking for you everywhere."

Eliza cursed and turned around, plastering a benign smile on her face. She had gotten distracted and given Aaron the opening. He looked handsome as ever standing before her, all broad shoulders and dark eyes and square, chiseled features. She had fallen for him so hard three years ago, at a party not dissimilar to this one. *Foolish girl*, she thought.

"Aaron," Eliza said. "A pleasure." She didn't reach out to shake his hand, and he didn't offer his.

Instead, Aaron looked a little pleading, a lot worried. So different than his usual blustering confidence. She could see a bead of sweat on one temple.

"I have to talk to you," Aaron said, with a smile that turned into a grimace.

"We're talking," Eliza said coolly. "Have you seen Whitney yet? And Becks?"

Aaron glanced behind him. "Becks should be here any minute, I'm sure. Why? You're not doing a story on him?"

Eliza felt a rush of righteous indignation. "Absolutely not. I promised Whitney. You know I'd never..." She shook her head. "Besides, if they should be worried about anyone here tonight, it's the journalist skulking over there in the corner." She pointed to a small, beaver-faced young man taking a quick, self-conscious bite of the candied nuts, little eyes darting around as if expecting someone to protest.

Aaron barely gave the man a passing look. "Yes, I know, sorry, I just—I'm distracted. Can I talk to you? In private?"

"Is it about Becks?"

Aaron took a deep breath and sighed. "No. He's fine. This —this venture will be good for him. I'm proud of him."

Right. Eliza had heard Aaron's unfiltered opinion, back when the scandal had happened. Had watched him replay the horrendous tackle, over and over, showing how Becks could have played it differently, implicating Becks in what came after.

"Is it about Gina?" Eliza said.

Aaron winced. "No, of course not. That was one night, Eliza. Please, just for five minutes. Come with me."

"Well, if it isn't my favorite football player!" Gina Tiller said, voice needling, as she sidled up to Aaron. Her creamy, peach skin looked shockingly pale against Aaron's dark ebony. "How are you doing, handsome? Oh, Eliza—how are you?" And she slipped one arm through Aaron's, which he shook off by patting her awkwardly on the shoulder instead. Unde-terred, Gina reached out to hug Eliza, and Eliza stiffened as her arms mechanically accepted it. *Why did you do that,* she chastised herself. *You should have turned your shoulder to her.*

"What do you think of all this?" Gina asked, her eyes slip-ping greedily from Aaron to Eliza. Her strawberry gold hair was pulled back into a tight bun, capped with a ridiculous red flower. "So exciting, isn't it? Poor Becks, he deserves some good fortune, after everything. I heard he is giving a portion of the profits to Eggertson's family. You know, for physical therapy and the like. Though I don't really know how you can give physical therapy to someone who's paralyzed."

Eliza stared at her, stricken.

"Ah, well," Aaron said, embarrassed for her, "there's actually a lot to do. Strength training, stretching, exercises—"

"Yeah, but he'll never walk again," Gina said, making a brushing-away motion with her hand. "He'll always be in a wheelchair."

"Excuse me," Eliza said. "Whitney just arrived. I should go say hi. No, stay," she said, as Aaron moved to join her. "I'm sure you two have plenty to catch up on."

"Oh, absolutely!" Gina said, threading her arm through Aaron's again and letting off a high-pitched cackle.

Someone, Eliza thought, *should do the world a favor and push Gina Tiller off a cliff.*

CHAPTER 4

$\mathcal{W}$hitney Becker clung close to her husband's shoulder as they made the rounds. She tired of the falsely sweet voices saying, *Oh, Becks, so fantastic to see you!* and *Looking good, Becks! Proud of you, man.* She trusted none of them. She knew that the invitees were either friends of Evan's or acquaintances who had come to gawk and see what the scandal had done to the once-famous lineman.

Whitney was many things, but a fool was not one of them. She steered her husband through the introductions, smiled where necessary, and drew him slowly, inexorably, over to where Evan stood, talking to an older gentleman with a blue handkerchief in his suit pocket.

"The guest of honor!" Evan cried, excusing himself to the older gentleman. "Becks! Whit!" He shook Becks' hand with great vigor and gave Whitney a tepid hug.

Whitney glanced at Becks, scrutinizing him, relaxing as a genuine smile spread across his face. Evan could do that to him—Evan was the one person who could make Becks forget himself for a moment, and genuinely enjoy himself. Even Whitney had lost the ability to do that.

"Nice party," Becks said. "How much of the seed money is going towards it?"

Evan laughed uproariously—too much, in Whitney's opinion. But Becks grinned back, and Whitney even gave him an answering smile. The answer was that of course none of the seed money had gone into the party, though who knew what credit cards Evan had tapped to throw it. The money would officially be transferred into Becker & Miller Associates tomorrow, after Evan and Becks signed, with a flourish, the contract in front of the gathered crowd. All silliness, in Whitney's opinion, but Evan had insisted that their kind of business relied on publicity and word of mouth, and such stunts were absolutely necessary.

"I need to introduce you to a few folks," Evan said, clapping Becks on the back. "Some interested investors."

"Already?"

"Ab-so-lutely."

"Do they know this business is just run by a dumb football player and his crazy friend?"

Evan's grin widened. "I'm really pumping up the whole *accountant plus celebrity* model, you know."

"Disgraced celebrity," Becks said, and the mood turned awkward. Evan took a quick swig of his drink. "I'll be right back," Becks continued. "Going to use the bathroom."

"How's your headache?" Whitney said sharply, and Becks scowled at her, withdrawing his arm.

"Fine."

"Do you want me to come with you?"

"No. I'll be fine."

"Do you need an aspirin?"

"No."

Whitney bit her tongue to keep from asking yet another question. She couldn't baby him, not too much. His resentment of her would only grow. Evan reassured Becks he would be right there when he came back and then turned towards Whitney.

"You, ah, look nice," he said awkwardly.

Whitney just gave him a scathing look. "Are all the papers in order?"

"Yes, of course."

"Are you sure? Because if—"

"Whitney, yes. I triple-checked. Come on, enjoy yourself. Have a glass of champagne."

Whitney shuddered. "I can't. I'm too nervous."

"Why?"

"I don't know. I feel like—I just have this sense that *something* is going to go wrong."

"Stop. You're just getting in your head. Leave the paranoia to Becks."

She shot another warning look, and Evan held up his hands.

"Sorry," he said quickly. "Bad joke. I just mean, everything is fine. You don't have to worry."

"I just want this night to be over."

Evan scowled. "Don't worry, it will be. Soon. Just—enjoy yourself in the meantime, okay? When's the last time you've really been out, out like this? De-stress a little. Have a cocktail. Mingle."

"That's not exactly *de-stressing*."

He raised an eyebrow at her, and Whitney shook her head in annoyance, a lock of hair tumbling across her face. She had to stay focused tonight, make sure everything ran smoothly, make sure Becks was exactly where he needed to be.

"There is...one thing I wanted to mention," Evan said, tugging at his ear.

"What?"

"It's not a problem. Don't look at me like that. It's handled."

"What's the problem?"

"Whit—don't panic. I wasn't even going to tell you."

"Tell me."

Evan sucked in a long breath. "It's just—people talk, you know?"

Whitney's stomach flipped. "Daniel," she said. Her eyes roved the room for him, and her heart began to race wildly. "I need to find Daniel."

"Wait! Whit. Hold on, it's not—"

But she left him, pulse pounding in her ears. *Daniel*, she thought, heart lurching. She had to get to him.

Because what if someone had told him the one thing she couldn't bear for him to hear?

CHAPTER 5

*G*ina Tiller was not one to mind going where she was not wanted.

Part of it was the pure pleasure of defiance—of seeing the fear or animosity or trepidation in someone's eyes, and knowing that they didn't have the courage to confront her. Part of it was pure indifference to others' feelings about her: Gina had enough money to know that she would always be wanted *somewhere*, and didn't have any of that nasty insecurity of those born into poverty, which Gina defined as anything less than six figures a year (per person in the household, of course).

So when Evan Tiller moved up to the front of the room to give a speech, Gina started to sidle her way to the stage.

The party really *was* a much larger affair than she had thought it would be. Indeed, Gina had only accepted Evan's lukewarm invitation to join in order to have a few drinks and marvel at the misery of the disgraced ex-football player trying to open a business with his high school buddy. But the party was tastefully done—she would give Evan that—and it turned out that he had drawn quite the crowd of St. Clair socialites, including a rather drunk Paulette McKenzie, who was hanging like a leech on the arm of the rather flustered and rather flattered Mr. Walpoe, an old bachelor who resembled a stretched-out frog.

Even the decorations were tasteful: not garish football colors and blown-up posters of Daniel Becker, as Gina had expected, but gold and red sashes and rugs and even themed drinks, served in fine crystal cocktail glasses. A plated dinner would have been nice, of course, but then, Gina couldn't expect someone like Evan Miller, living off of the investment of his more successful best friend, to afford that.

"Ahem," Evan said, tapping the microphone. The crowd's humming gradually ceased, and bodies turned towards the front of the stage. Only Gina continued to move through them, sidestepping men in suits and women in pastel dresses and waiters with their stiff ties and stiffer manners. "Everyone can hear me?"

A few hearty cheers.

"Fantastic!" Evan grinned. He seemed easy in front of a crowd, Gina thought. Nothing like the nervous, shy Becks. Gina could remember Becks when he was recruited just after college. She had been twenty-five then and loved to (as she still did) sort through every photo of every new recruit, ranking them in order of attractiveness. Becks had been near the top: tall, with a square jaw that undid his otherwise pretty-boy face, and bright green eyes flecked with brown. He had been so *nice*, too, when Gina had met him at the first banquet her father held. Too bad for that damn girlfriend—she certainly had known a good thing when she saw it, and made sure to get a ring from Becks within his first year of professional football. And, wonder of all wonders, Becks was one of those rare unicorns who was too ethical or too cowardly to cheat.

Evan was saying something now about how he had always hoped to run a business with Becks, how they complemented each other, and *blah blah blah*. Then he waved towards the front of the crowd, and Becks, nudged by his wife Whitney, took a tentative step towards the stage's stairs. The crowd began to cheer. Gina joined in, clapping, that same serpentine smile plastered on her face. *Poor Becks*, she thought. She wondered if the rumors about CTE were true. *Chronic traumatic encephalopathy.* Nasty name. Her father never liked talking about it. "I smell a lawsuit!" he would say, and that would be that. People were always trying to sue you when you were rich.

"And I just want to add," Evan said, "that I've never been more proud to be your friend, Becks. Seriously. In every situation you've ever been in, you've handled yourself with grace, courage, and strength. I'm so lucky to have you, and I can only have the highest hopes for Becker & Miller knowing that you're a part of it. So with that said," Evan concluded, raising his glass. The crowd cheered again. Gina began to ascend the steps. "With that said—" Evan glanced once, then twice, at Gina, his eyes widening, panic creeping into his expression. Gina grinned. "Here's a toast, to Becks! And Becker & Miller!"

A cheers, dulled somewhat by the surprise of seeing Gina on stage. But the crowd followed Evan's example and downed their champagne. Becks looked awkward, like an animal off-leash. He had no drink in his hand: no doubt Whitney had put a stop to any of that, at least until the doctors gave him the all-clear. Which, in Gina's limited experience, would be never. Didn't they say, after all, that the only time you could actually prove CTE was after death?

"Hello!" Gina said, tugging the microphone from Evan's fingers. That was his first mistake, letting her have it. He was probably hoping she wasn't going to make a scene, had probably weighed his options and decided that the path of least resistance was best.

The crowd quieted. She could see the faces looking up at her with confusion and mild interest. Gina grinned. She still felt a mild buzz from the last gin and tonic she had had—her fourth or fifth, but who was counting?

"Hello," Gina said. "Thank you for coming to the *wonderful* event put on by my *great* friend Evan Miller, and of course, the *wonderful* Daniel Becker." She clapped her hands, and the crowd, wincing at the loud sounds that echoed through the speakers, joined in after a few seconds, haltingly.

"Gina," Evan said, smiling and drawing nearer. "Did you—?"

"I just wanted to say a few words of congratulations," Gina said, twisting away from him. "Evan is a really stand-up guy. And I mean *stand-up*." She could feel Evan really starting to panic behind her, coming close enough that Gina felt sure he meant to try and reach for the microphone. She took another step away and began pacing the stage. "Isn't that so, Evan? Haven't you always been a stand-up guy?"

Evan gave a pale smile. Becks look inquisitively at her.

"I mean, using your rich friend's money to start a new business!" Gina said. "Brilliant! Wonderful career move!"

The whispers started, rolling across the crowd. Gina relished them. She felt intoxicated—she always did when she was in front of a crowd. It was a particular weakness that her father had learned to manage, or circumvent.

"But that's not all you've been scheming up, is it?" Gina said, whipping on Evan. He looked white, whether from fear or embarrassment, Gina didn't know. She didn't care. "Want to tell us what else you have in store for us, Evan? For Becks here?"

She waited, twirling the microphone in one hand. A man like Evan Miller was really nothing more than a sad little upstart. A man who would announce a partnership with a celebrity widely believed to have CTE, a celebrity whose career had ended in the most horrible, spectacular fashion six months ago. Because he needed Becks to be something, anything. And he was willing to do whatever he needed to in order to make that happen.

Gina might have admired it—but then, she was rich enough to have higher moral standards. *She* would never scheme or plot to make money, and if this was only because she had enough of it to last her ten lifetimes, she didn't particularly care. What she did care about was watching the panic twist and warp Evan's face. He should have been nicer to her, should have greeted her when she came to the party that night, should have treated her like the special guest of honor that she was. He hadn't, of course, and she had been reduced to wandering the party on her own, to listening to the conversations of strangers around her, to talking to half-acquaintances with silly pleasantries.

If he *had* bothered to talk to her, though, she might have missed one of the most important conversations of the night. The one that she was *really* dying to tell.

Patience, she counseled herself.

Evan snatched the microphone back from her, obviously catching Gina's moment of distraction. She didn't care; she had finished her job for the night, and gave him a sly smile as he began speaking into the microphone, stuttering over himself. "Ah, thanks Gina, for that...anyway. Please enjoy the drinks and the food, and if I haven't had a chance to say hello, please find me. I want to thank each and every one of you for coming. Becks and I both do."

"And Whitney, of course," Gina said, loud enough to be picked up by the microphone. "Can't forget Whitney, sweet little snake that she is."

Becks' head whipped round to her. Gina knew she shouldn't have said this last part; nothing lost a crowd like insulting a well-liked woman, especially a woman so nobly hitched to a tragic figure. But what did she care? She wanted another gin and tonic.

"I'll talk to you later," she said to Becks, winking at him.

He stared at her, naked dislike on his face. For a moment it chilled Gina; she sobered up for an instant and even blushed to look out at the dozens upon dozens of eyes on her. But then she shook herself and walked off stage.

She wasn't done with her good deeds for the night.

CHAPTER 6

"I'm so sorry," Evan repeated, as he huddled with Whitney and Becks a few moments later. Becks looked ill and kept rubbing his temples, while Whitney's lips were pressed in a thin line.

"We should go soon," Whitney said. "Becks isn't feeling well, anyway."

"Not yet," Evan said sharply.

Whitney glared at him. Evan met her stare with one of his own. He was going into business with her husband, yes, but they both knew that essentially meant he was going into business with Whitney. And she needed to understand when to listen to him—to see reason.

"We have to talk through something," Evan said, voice tight. "And besides that, Becks still needs to sign the contract."

Whitney huffed at this. Becks *did* look out of it, sometimes massaging his temples, sometimes looking about him with the air of a baffled child. Evan felt a wave of pity for his friend, so strong that it almost knocked him to his knees. He could help him, he thought. Make him better. If they took a trip for a little while, got away from all this…

But it was too late.

It had been too late for years.

"Fine," Whitney said, her voice just as tight. "Fifteen more minutes. That's it."

Evan nodded, swallowing hard.

He had to play this right.

CHAPTER 7

"*D*isgusting," Eliza said, and the girl standing next to her outside the restroom nodded, all righteous indignation and horror at Gina's outburst. It was easy to hate a rich, spoiled girl like Gina, and it felt rather nice sharing in the hatred with a pleasant stranger. The toilet flushed, and a bird-like woman emerged, adjusting her satin dress with a glazed look in her eyes. The agreeable girl disappeared inside, and Eliza sighed, leaning up against the wallpaper and wishing she had not quit cigarettes earlier that month.

"Eliza."

Eliza whipped around to see Aaron standing there, looking undone. She straightened, heart picking up a beat. But she managed, coolly enough, "What do you want, Aaron?"

"I need to talk to you. I need your help."

"Embarrassed about your girlfriend's performance?"

Aaron only shut his eyes and squeezed them. The movement was so unlike him that Eliza stepped forward, brows knitting. "Aaron?" she said. "Are you going to faint?"

"Please," Aaron said, between tightened lips. "Please come talk to me."

Eliza followed Aaron out of the room. Fifteen minutes

later, she emerged, pale and shaken and grim, Aaron close at her heels.

"Thank you," Aaron said. "Thank you, Eliza. I know I don't deserve your help, but—"

"Shh," Eliza said. "Not here."

"But you *will* help me?"

She gave him a scathing look. "Yes, you idiot," she said. "Of course I will."

All the while, her stomach kept sinking down, down, down.

CHAPTER 8

*R*ick Fales stood at the corner of the banquet hall, or ballroom, or whatever those stupid rich folks called the football-field-sized recreational room used for entertaining in the mansion. It had been the worst sort of night: he had not gotten close enough to Becks to get a quote, no one who recognized him would talk to him, and worst of all, he couldn't find the one person who had made the evening interesting, Gina Tiller. Each person Rick asked about her seemed to have a different account of where the socialite had gone.

He knew that Evan Miller had invited him in the hopes he might do a little write-up on the new company, might generate some business for the nascent venture Becker & Miller. It was a risky move, one that Rick could admire—he could just as easily write an article about how disoriented Daniel Becker seemed that night, which indeed he planned to do, provided he couldn't work in anything of the Gina angle.

In the meantime, he snatched champagne off of every tray of every waiter that sashayed by, mentally calculating the money that went into such a party. Rick had never catered a party in his life: even his wedding had been a slipshod affair, where his wife—who was far too sensible a woman to stay married to him, ultimately—had kept a tight fist over the budget, insisting that they host the reception at their crumbling apartment and snapping at every great-aunt that dared comment about the lack of food options or the beer-and-wine-only bar service.

Yes, Rick had only ever brushed shoulders with wealth such as this, and it simultaneously fascinated him and made him nauseous. He knew these people felt they were better than him, maybe not consciously, but in their bones. He knew that they lived on another plane entirely, fussing over dress appointments and boarding schools and Christmas party invitations and ski vacations. They were the kind of people who would insist that they were "tightening their budget" for a year and meant only that they were taking one less vacation, or the kind who would declare themselves in "financial crisis" when they had only to draw from little Timothy's trust fund to make things right again. None of *them* had driven for a ride-sharing app on cold winter nights in order to make the heat bill that month. None of *them* had hawked watches and boots and anything else they could find to pay for a wedding ring, or donated plasma until their arm was bruised and sore to afford the plumber bill.

Yes, these were the kind of people who held themselves above everyone else, and for good reason—Rick would give them that. He had no misconceptions: he would give his right arm to be one of them. But he wasn't. He was a journalist, and an ill-liked one at that. Sure, sometimes he freelanced for some of the big guys, but his best client was a gossip magazine, and that was exactly who would be receiving his article tonight. If Evan Miller was too stupid to realize that this was a possibility, well, then that was his problem. At least Rick had shown up—he was sure half a dozen other reporters had not, deciding not to touch the Daniel Becker storyline with a ten-foot pole.

That was the tragic part of it all, really. The poor, injured, likely brain-damaged football player being dragged around to shake hands and pretend that yes, he was going to be a full partner in the firm, when really his best friend was just trying to get a profitable new venture going, and his wife was just trying to figure out a way to provide for them now that the football money had dried up. *That* was the story that Rick was going to tell.

In a sad way, he actually felt kind of let down by Daniel Becker. He had always liked the guy, as much as he liked any athlete. He was shy, slow-spoken, but not unintelligent. He didn't drive a fancy sports car or date models or party down in Miami, as almost all of the other predictable football players did. The one time that Rick had interviewed him, out at a playoff party, the athlete known as Becks had even treated him with a modicum of decency—had offered to refill his drink, had confessed he wasn't a huge fan of parties, and had even asked Rick's advice on talking to the press, as if Rick was a human being, as if he had real thoughts inside his head other than just worshipping the stars around him.

That collision, though—that had been brutal. Like everyone else in the nation, Rick had watched it over two dozen times, at every kind of speed. A routine tackle, except that Becks had dipped his shoulder, had clenched his fist, in such a way as to cause total and absolute devastation. It was hard to come back from that, not even counting the swift and brutal penalties imposed on him by the NFL.

Had CTE really caused the sudden burst of violence? Or was it adrenaline, just run haywire? Was Becks doping, as some pundits alleged—even though all of his tests, including a blood test ordered as soon as the game had finished, were clean? Rick didn't know. But based on the way Becks was acting tonight, his first night out in public since that horrible play, since retiring from the NFL, Rick was sure that things weren't looking good for the former football player.

Rick took yet another champagne flute off of a passing

tray. Was it his imagination, or did the waiter try to swivel the tray away and keep Rick from it? No matter. He downed it in two gulps, the buzz tingling through his fingertips. He would be out of here soon. He just needed one more good quote.

Miracle of miracles, he spotted Sam O'Nally in one corner of the room, alone. O'Nally was another disgraced football player, albeit for different reasons: he had retired a few years ago and descended quickly into alcoholism, becoming another football poster boy for CTE. Rick wasn't so sure about the conclusion. It seemed like all the players were quick to blame their problems on the illness that could not be proven. But, at least, O'Nally would be good for a quote.

"Enjoying the party?" Rick said, moving to the window ledge that O'Nally was leaning up against. The large ex-footballer jumped, then frowned down at Rick. O'Nally was a bear, a defensive end that seemed almost as wide as he was tall, with a swirl of ginger hair and a five o'clock shadow that, even in his playing days, he never seemed to shake.

"Fales," O'Nally said. "You're drunk."

"One to talk, eh?" Rick said. He resisted the urge to correct O'Nally—he so hated it when people just used his last name. Most of them did it to mock him, once they noticed the unfortunate homonym. "Must be a dull party without any booze."

O'Nally lifted one eyebrow. Rick could feel him weighing whether to even talk to him, or to turn back to his silent corner and keep stewing.

Rick decided to try to tip the scale in his favor. "I can grab you a drink, if you'd like," he said. "That way you don't have to order it. What will it be, whiskey? Double?"

"Screw off."

Rick blushed. Fine. The man could play it that way. Truth be told, Rick was relieved he hadn't said yes—he didn't like the idea of bringing an alleged alcoholic a drink. "Fine. Understandable. Well? And how are you enjoying the place?

Have you spoken to Becks? He invited you, I guess? Have you two been in touch since his retirement?" Drink made Rick's tongue loose, and it was with an effort that he shut his mouth.

"What's your angle, Fales? Want to talk about how two CTE losers were together at a party? Rag mags missing a few articles? Not enough affairs this time of year, eh?"

"I'm reporting on the opening of Becker & Miller."

"Bull." O'Nally gave him a sour look. "That's what I hate about you scumbags. You can't even admit you're not honest. At least there'd be some integrity in that."

"Fair, fair," Rick said jovially. "Well, I was *invited* here by Evan to write about that. But I'm just feeling things out, seeing if there's anything better out here."

"Like me."

"Not quite—no offense. I wanted to see how Becks was doing. And then Gina—well, that was something, wasn't it?"

O'Nally's face darkened at the woman's name, and Rick brightened with a sudden memory. "Of course," Rick said smoothly, "I can only imagine how it is for *you* to see her here. She made such a big fuss out of that little incident with you, didn't she? Ridiculous. It was obvious she was drunk on stage today. And what she said about Whitney—"

"Gina Tiller is absolute scum," O'Nally said, gnashing his teeth. "Put that in your article."

Rick nodded encouragingly and tried a few more times to elicit something else from O'Nally—though really, that was a good enough quote to run with, if he needed to. He watched O'Nally carefully as they spoke: could he see signs of CTE in him? Was that droop in his eyelids it, for instance? Or the sharp way that he talked? Or his anger towards Gina, even months later, even when it was O'Nally who had been at fault? He tried to see something of the disease on the man's face, in his body, in his movements. And there was decidedly something *off* about Sam O'Nally. Rick couldn't quite put his finger on it, but there was a reason the man was standing alone at the side of the room during a party. His every emotional current seemed to run back to anger.

And Becks? Was Becks the same? Rick glanced around, his eyes by chance locking on the tall, broad-shouldered figure of Daniel Becker. He had to talk to him. He had to know.

Daniel Becker looked up, for a moment meeting Rick's eyes.

CHAPTER 9

"They're talking about me," Becks said sadly.

"Who?" Whitney said, whipping around. "Oh, Sam? That's all right, honey, he's a friend."

"And the journalist."

"Journalist?" Whitney's voice was sharp, a little panicked. She set her champagne glass down on the table and squinted. "How do you know he's a journalist?"

"I've seen him before. Fales, I think his name is. He keeps looking over."

Whitney glanced over and sighed. "Daniel, he's not. He's talking to Sam."

"He was just a second ago."

She watched the journalist for a few more beats, fingers tapping on the sleeve of her dress. She was so beautiful, Becks thought. He wondered how hard the past few months had been for her. If Whitney had felt terribly the sudden transition from being the wife of a beloved football star to the wife of a disgraced one, she had not given any indication of it. "He's not," Whitney said flatly. "He hasn't looked over here once. You're being paranoid, honey."

Paranoia. Becks felt the hair on the back of his neck rise.

One of the hallmark signs of CTE. Whitney knew it too. Her eyes met his for a moment, and then looked away. "Maybe he did glance over for a second earlier," she said, offering them both an out. "But I wouldn't worry about it. Let's just wrap up with the party. Come on, Evan wanted to introduce you to someone before we go—"

"No," Becks said. "I'm—I'm going to use the bathroom."

"Again?"

Becks shrugged. "Been drinking a lot of water," he said, which was ridiculous—of course that wasn't it. He was feeling dizzy, though, dizzy and disoriented. He just wanted to sit down. For some reason that he couldn't pinpoint, rage was bubbling inside of him. It was all just so monstrously unfair. One tackle, one stupid, unfortunate tackle had landed him here. He knew that everyone thought that the way he had moved his shoulder had been intentional. He knew that it looked bad. He never even tried lending the explanation of what he had been thinking that day, of how the strange body movement had been due to hesitation rather than brute force. Who would believe him? Becks had seen the film—he certainly wouldn't, if anyone else said so.

And now he was here, being paraded around like a puppet and being forced to act nice while the big kids talked. He could see the way people looked at him, with that particular mixture of pity and fear in their eyes. Waiting for him to burst again. Waiting for him to break.

And that woman—Gina. She was worst of all. She had been leering at him as she spoke into the microphone, taking the moment that was supposed to be the start of Becks putting it all back together and ruining it. She insulted Evan, and she insulted Whitney, the two people who had been there for Becks when everything was falling apart. And what could he do? He didn't trust himself to try to talk to her, not with the way his mind was working. He would stumble over his words. He would grow flustered and stutter, and then Gina would cluck and touch his sleeve and say something condescending and sweet, just like the rest of them.

Becks needed to get out.

He tore through the rooms of the house, growing disoriented as he left the bright lights of the banquet hall and stumbled through the back kitchen, the atrium, and then some sort of giant two-storied living room with rich carpets and antique lamps. He couldn't tell if it was rage or heartburn bubbling in his core; it hurt, whatever it was, so much that Becks wanted to scream. Black spots danced at the corner of his vision; Becks' hands opened and then tightened into fists.

CHAPTER 10

*G*ina's father told her once that all men had secrets, and that you never truly had power over them until you knew one.

Except, Gina now knew two secrets—or maybe one big one—and she didn't like it, not at all. She had toyed with the idea of confronting the secret keepers, of publicly outing them, but even with her champagne buzz the idea didn't hold more than a passing fascination. The trouble was, secrets could also hurt. And Gina didn't like hurting people—at least, not to their face, not in a way that she would have to see and experience firsthand.

But that was no matter. She had figured out exactly what to do. She slipped out of the party, motioning to someone as she went. She climbed the stairs to the bedrooms of the East-wick mansion and chose one at random, delighted that it turned out to be the master. It had a balcony; it was cold, but Gina felt too hot anyway, and so she stepped out onto the little enclosure and lit a cigarette. *I really should quit,* she thought to herself, her sacred mantra every time she took that first drag.

"Gina."

Gina's lip curled into a half-smile, but she didn't turn around.

"I'm disappointed in you," she said, tapping out ashes over the railing. "I'm going to give you a chance to make it right, of course."

Silence. Gina took another drag of her cigarette and let out her breath in soft *O*s. Of course what she said might sound cryptic—might even sound as if she wished for money, or to somehow extort someone. But that wasn't it at all. For once in her life, Gina felt she had the moral ground. There was something intoxicating in that, actually. She felt quite the good person—perhaps she might try it more often.

"Don't worry," Gina said, sighing into the cold night. "I'll give you a little time. Because if you don't—well, I'll be forced to say something, of course. I think that's pretty obvious." She thought about what else she might add, words about fairness and justice and mercy, pretty words that she was too drunk to put together right now. Perhaps she could call and say them tomorrow.

"That's fair," the voice said, and Gina nodded. It was fair. *She* was fair. And quite noble, really, to be forcing someone's hand like this. She took a deep breath. Maybe from this day forward, she would be good. She would live her life doing favors for others, doling out good deeds, enjoying the fruits of her kindness and generosity. She would be like Mother Theresa, except...well, she didn't actually know much about Mother Theresa, but people seemed to look up to her. Something about orphans, maybe? Gina would be like that.

She heard the footsteps approaching softly. For a moment her mind sharpened; the drunkenness faded away. *Danger*, her body warned, and for a brief, terrible moment, she had clarity: she should never be threatening someone with this kind of secret, never be making demands of them, and good God, *not from a balcony*.

She fought as best she could, but the struggle lasted only seconds.

And then Gina Tiller tipped over the edge of the railing and toppled three stories to the concrete pool deck below.

CHAPTER 11

*R*ick Fales heard something like a great crash and froze. He was in a part of the house he shouldn't have been in, after following Daniel Becker through the back kitchen and promptly losing him. He wondered if something had fallen off the stage at the party, or whether, God forbid, someone was ransacking the mansion.

In the dark rooms, lit only by nightlights, Rick felt something like fear. Everything seemed sinister in deep shadow: Rick kept feeling as though he were spotting someone or something out of the corner of his eye, but when he turned, nothing would be there. He had heard accounts of the creepiness of St. Clair before he had moved in and had always chalked up the stories to local legend. But he was close to the lake now, closer than he had ever been, and could feel some of the dark magic washing over him.

Or perhaps he had just had too much to drink.

Finally, Rick screwed up the courage to venture upstairs, the only other place that he could conceive Becks to have gone. He rounded the corner to one of the stone staircases and leapt back, letting out a cry.

The figure slumped across the stairs stirred and groaned, but continued to sleep.

"Becks?" Rick whispered. He gave the sleeping body a nudge. "Becks! What are you doing?"

The ex-football player yawned, his body awkwardly attempting to curl itself close as it lay draped over the hard, gray stones. Rick poked him with the corner of his foot. "Becks! Daniel! Wake up!"

Rick leaned forward to see if he could smell alcohol on the man—nothing. Just as he was leaning back, though, Becks' eyes flew open, and one hand shot out to grab Rick's collar.

"Take it easy!" Rick squealed. "I-I mean, take it easy, man. You were sleeping. I'm just waking you up."

Becks was breathing heavily, chest rising and falling, eyes wide and haunted. His hand was shaking, Rick realized. Had it always been?

"You okay?" Rick said, gently trying to pry off Becks' fingers. The ex-footballer let him, and Rick took a quick step back, massaging his throat and taking deep gulps of air.

"Where am I?" Becks said, blinking up at Rick.

Rick's stomach flipped. "You're at the Eastwick mansion. We're having your party. You know, Becker & Miller? Big money? You and your buddy Evan, hamming it up with all these rich folks?"

Becks blinked at Rick. Rick felt another stab of panic.

"The Eastwick mansion," Becks repeated.

"Yes."

"I shouldn't be over here," Becks said. "I was just—I was so angry—"

"Parties will do that to you," Rick said, aiming for lightness. "Hey, while I have you here, I'm actually working on a story—"

But Becks didn't seem to hear him. He rose, blinking, and Rick took another step back. He forgot just how large football players were until he stood in front of them: it was sometimes like they were gods from another world, come to live among mortals. Except, Becks was a fallen god now.

"What am I doing," Becks said, pressing the heels of his hands into his temples. "I was just—I came over here, and —and—"

Rick heard shouts, building in volume from some other part of the mansion. Not the banquet hall, but the backyard, it seemed. He wondered if people were dipping in the pool—a bad idea in winter, a worse idea when drunk.

"I wouldn't worry about it," Rick said with faux cheerfulness. "We all need to get away from parties sometimes. So, I was wondering, if you could just answer one question I have —namely, how you feel about this new venture, in light of everything else going on?"

Jeez, why was he so nervous? Rick couldn't stop his voice from squeaking again near the end. He sounded like a frightened schoolboy. But it was the look in Becks' eyes that terrified him, the frightened look of a wounded animal, trying desperately to make sense of his new reality. Rick shuddered.

"New venture," Becks repeated.

The shouts grew louder. Rick glanced over at them, frowning, and then jumped when the door to the backyard burst open.

"9-1-1!" a woman shouted. Eliza Vorne. "Someone call 9-1-1!" She cursed as she sprinted across the flagstones of the house, repeating her message until she was in the brightly lit banquet hall. Rick felt the hush fall over the room, the way the low buzz of voices died down into something horrible and still.

"What happened?" Becks asked, and Rick turned back to him. The footballer looked pale and frightened. "Who's hurt?"

"It might be nothing," Rick found himself saying, ridiculously. "Maybe a fire, or something got stolen, or—"

"Is she dead?" one of the guests said, loudly, following the frazzled Eliza back through the mansion and out towards the backyard. "No vital signs?"

"How should I know!" Eliza wailed. "Hurry!"

Next to Rick, Becks began to shake.

CHAPTER 12

*G*ina Tiller was dead—undeniably.

Eliza watched as the doctor crouched to her side, reeling back as soon as she could make out the awful stillness of Gina's figure, the strange tilt of her neck. The doctor gingerly pressed her fingers against the woman's throat, feeling for a pulse, but withdrew it seconds later with a quick shake of her head.

"She fell from there?" the doctor said, pointing to the balcony above. Next to her, Aaron shuddered and pulled Eliza closer, and this time, she didn't pull away. "It's not that far a fall. It was the landing...she might have survived it, if she had fallen differently."

Thanks, Eliza felt like saying. *I'll be sure to convey that to the family.* But instead she said nothing, pressing her face against Aaron's chest, trying to drown out the image of that horrible...*thing*...on the pool deck.

"The police are on their way," Eliza muttered into Aaron's suit jacket. He was the first to hear the crash, the first to raise the alarm. *Oh, God*, Eliza thought. It was all just too terrible.

"We should probably get going," Aaron said.

"Shouldn't we wait to talk to them?"

"No, baby. Not a good idea."

"Don't call me baby," Eliza said automatically. She looked up at Aaron, tilting her head far back. "Do you think—do you think that—"

"Shh," Aaron said. "Let's go. It'll all be all right." The doctor stood behind them, awkward and uncertain now that there was nothing for her to do. In the distance, Eliza could hear sirens.

"You don't know what I was going to ask."

"I do, baby—I mean, Eliza. I know. Don't worry about it. Just look at me, huh? It'll all be all right."

That was when Eliza burst into tears.

CHAPTER 13

"*D*aniel," Whitney said sharply. "Where's Daniel?"

Her search for him had proven fruitless, and she had eventually returned to the main room, trembling after one last unpleasant errand. The night was not going anything like she had hoped—and Whitney had certainly had low expectations to begin with.

Evan was there in the banquet hall, still making the rounds, shaking all of the hands of potential donors. But now Whitney heard sirens in the distance, and her first impulse was to grab onto her husband and hold.

But where was he?

"Whitney," Evan said sharply. But Whitney pushed her way past their small group, depositing her champagne glass on the nearest table with a careless gesture that sent liquid spilling over her hand. She followed the voices and the lights; for a moment, she felt as though she were floating. A strange sense of unreality took over her.

Whitney pushed her way through the glass doors and out onto the back patio. A police officer said something to her. Something like *stop, ma'am, please, police line*, but Whitney was barely listening. She saw the figure sprawled out on the stones, and for one horrible second her mind stuttered, and she thought it might be Daniel. Then she took a few steps closer, and the twisted figure of Gina Tiller was visible, still and pale in the moonlight.

Hands closed around her arms, dragging her back. Whitney gulped in air. *He did this for me*, she thought wildly. *He did this for me, and I have to protect him.*

CHAPTER 14

"*Y*ou okay?" Rick said, eyeing the still-shaking Becks. He wondered if he needed to call a paramedic over to tend to the ex-footballer.

"D-dead?" Becks said, and he looked up at Rick with such a confused, dismayed expression, that Rick was tempted to pat Becks on the shoulder like a child, and tell him that all would be fine.

"Gina Tiller," Rick said instead. "Sounds like she took a tumble off a balcony upstairs." It had been easy enough to hear that through the shouts and the police radioing each other incessantly. "Were you upstairs at the time? Did you see anything?"

Becks just looked bewildered. Rick felt a twist in his stomach. What if….But he didn't want it to be true.

"Daniel!"

Whitney Becker sprinted across the hall and into her husband's arms. Becks rose just in time to catch her, and the two of them all but tumbled to the stairs behind them. Rick stood a few feet away, awkward and hesitating. He *should* leave the married couple to talk things out, he knew. But still, there was the opportunity for one more quote…

"Daniel, where were you?" Whitney said, sobbing into his coat jacket. Becks held her, still looking bewildered. "Tell me. Daniel, tell me, where were you tonight? I couldn't find you."

"I-I fell asleep."

"Where? Here?" Whitney glanced around, eyes wet with tears. "On the *stairs*, Daniel?"

"I don't remember. I-I suppose so."

Whitney held him tighter. Rick felt the knot in his stomach twist further. He felt, truthfully, as though he might be a little sick.

"Daniel," Whitney said. She seemed not to have noticed Rick. "You must not say anything to the police. Do you understand? We're going to get a lawyer for you. A good one. You can't tell the police anything."

"What would I tell them?"

Whitney stifled a sob and pressed her cheek into her husband's chest. Becks rubbed the back of her shoulder, squeezing his own eyes shut.

"They can't prove anything," she said fiercely. And then she straightened, and jumped as she noticed Rick. "How long have you been standing there?" she demanded.

"Rick Fales, ma'am. I was just sitting here with your husband."

"Sitting with him? For how long?"

"Just the past ten minutes or so. We've been chatting."

"He doesn't talk to reporters."

"Oh, hardly anything on the record, ma'am, of course."

Whitney hesitated. "Ten minutes. Just…ten minutes?"

"Thereabouts."

"Did you see anything? Hear anything?"

She wanted to know if Rick could exculpate Becks. He could not. "Didn't hear or see anything out of the ordinary," Rick said. "Until someone started shouting about a body."

Whitney shuddered.

"One question, for a piece tomorrow?" Rick said hopefully. "What are—"

"No comment," Whitney said. She looked up at him, sharply and venomously, as if he were the worst kind of vermin that had scurried across her path. Rick shrugged sheepishly and took a few skulking steps away. He ran over and over in his head the image of Whitney's tear-filled eyes, the sound of her panicked words.

He wondered if he could trust his instincts.

Because he thought that Whitney Becker was hiding something.

CHAPTER 15

"What time is physical therapy?" Eliza asked. She was standing in Aaron's high-rise downtown apartment, with its river view and white marble floors and quartz countertops. It had been so long since she had been here—months, at least. He had gotten a new bamboo plant, which charmed Eliza until she realized that the stupid thing had probably been a gift from one of his lovers.

"Not for another hour. Sit down, Lize. You're making me dizzy."

She did, still frowning. Aaron sat at one of the high silver barstools, a plate of eggs and sausage before him. He had offered to cook some for Eliza, too, but she had demurred. It would be a long time before Eliza enjoyed any breakfast of Aaron's again.

She had agreed to come home with him the night before, though she had been extremely rigid on her rules: he was to take the couch, she was to shower alone in the morning, and he was not to make any moves on her, now or in the future. She was simply here to help.

Aaron, for his part, seemed more at ease than he had been

last night, as if a woman had not died, as if his major problem was just a few action steps away from being solved. Eliza didn't know how he did it. She suspected that all men were able to relax when they had a woman to pawn their problems off on, a woman who would fuss and schedule and plan and take away all need for them to busy their pretty little heads about it.

And fuss Eliza was. She had been working all morning on an action plan, and had presented it to Aaron with cool matter-of-factness. He had approved it while sipping black coffee and then changed the subject to that day's weather, as if one could follow naturally from the other.

"You don't seem to be taking this seriously," Eliza said.

"What? Of course I am."

"This is serious, Aaron."

"I'm well aware of that."

"I don't know if we can fix this in time."

"But we're trying. Right?" Aaron smiled at her. She fought the urge to roll her eyes. Where was the terrified man of the night before, the one begging her for a few minutes of her time, the one pleading with her to get her to help him, just once more? "Sorry, babe—I mean, Lize. I take it seriously, I do. I just—I'm thinking about some other things."

"Like the weather."

Aaron shook his head. He put his gold-plated fork down— a ridiculous utensil, Eliza thought, one of his more bone-headed purchases before Eliza had met him and could tell him that such frivolous things made him look immature. "Last night," he said. "That woman. Gina."

Eliza's stomach flipped. "Please," she said. "I don't want to talk about her."

Eliza knew all that she needed to know about the woman, and she didn't want to know more. She didn't want to have to sympathize with her, to think about her family, to consider that Gina Tiller might have been more than just a 2-D cut-out of a villain, a caricature of a society girl gone wrong.

She had found out about Gina Tiller and Aaron through a fluke. Eliza and Aaron had been having one of their well-trodden fights. The subject of it was embarrassing enough that Eliza was vague on details with her family: in truth, they had been arguing about whether their unborn, yet-to-be-conceived children would be allowed to play football, given the possibility of head injuries. Eliza was decidedly arguing against it; Aaron insisted that a more balanced approach was appropriate, letting the children weigh the pros and cons themselves.

"Children cannot make Venn diagrams of life decisions!" Eliza had shrieked, and had stormed out of this very apartment that she now stood in. She had slammed the door particularly hard, hoping that it would dislodge one of Aaron's expensive paintings, and stomped down to the parking garage. Aaron did not follow her, though he usually did. He did not text her, even though Eliza had stayed up until one a.m. that night waiting for the apology, the reconciliation.

By morning, Eliza was out for blood. She told Aaron that they were done with each other until further notice. He responded only with a thumbs up, which infuriated her. She decided then and there that she was done with him for good. Their four-year, on-again, off-again relationship was too embarrassing, Eliza decided. She was sick of not being able to make it work, of having to explain to everyone else what the current status of her relationship was. She was going to leave Aaron for good and move on with her life. At least, that had been her intention.

One week later, Eliza found herself driving to Aaron's place. She had cooled off considerably since their fight; she had even begun to think that perhaps she had been too harsh. She would apologize to Aaron for her behavior; he would accept her apology, of course he would, and they would try to move forward. Differently, of course. Better. Eliza might suggest something drastic like moving in, a new phase in their relationship that would mean new responsibilities and duties.

Except, when Eliza arrived at Aaron's place, she found more than she had bargained for. She found proof of *recent relations*, as she later told her mother, in Aaron's wastepaper basket. She confronted him when he got home (Aaron had forgotten, as he always did, that he had given her a spare key), and it took an interrogation of nearly an hour to get him to simply admit that yes, he had been with someone in the week since they had broken up. Eliza flew into a rage, and even more so when she realized that Aaron did not intend to divulge the name.

"It's someone I know!" she had cried, sobbing. "It's one of my friends, isn't it?"

But Eliza was not to be kept in suspense for very long. Two days later, she had run into Gina Tiller at the athletic club downtown. Gina caught her eyes, and a fat cat smile played over her face. Eliza knew then. But she walked right up to Gina and asked—"Aaron and you?" Gina had giggled— giggled!—and said that a lady never told. Eliza wanted to slap her. Instead she said, "I hope he told you that he has crabs," and walked off. Eliza hoped that Gina spent a fortune in medical bills and time in disproving the accusation. She hoped that Gina texted Aaron in a panic afterwards.

"We don't have to talk much," Aaron said now, carefully. "I just wanted to check that you were okay…with all of it."

"With all of what?" Eliza snapped. "The fact that she died or the fact that you slept with her? I'm not particularly fine with anything, you know."

Aaron watched her, carefully studying her face. Eliza blushed.

"I love you, Lize. You know that."

"We're not talking about love right now," Eliza said. "Get dressed. We're leaving for physical therapy."

He nodded at her, and Eliza's stomach flipped. She had the sinking feeling that perhaps he was not telling her everything.

Then again, neither was she.

CHAPTER 16

*R*ick Fales left his editor's office feeling troubled.

He had turned in his exclusive piece about the mysterious death of Gina Tiller, of course—with some nice, colorful details about the food, the guest list, the numerous tragedies of the Eastwick mansion.

"But there's nothing in here about Becks!" his editor had cried, exasperated. She was a leather-skinned woman of fifty-six, always dressed in a sharp suit, with designer glasses and cheap acrylic nails. "You can't write a story and not mention Becks. Why did I send you out there?"

"I actually pitched the story to you."

His editor had thrown her hands up. "Look, Rick, you want us to keep buying things from you? Keep focused."

"But I am! It's just that this girl Gina—"

"Died tragically, I know. Probably too much alcohol. She was always a partier, wasn't she?"

His editor got that comically hungry look on her face that she always did whenever anyone in the shadow of celebrity or wealth was mentioned. Rick privately thought it was what had drawn her into the gossip mags to begin with, though he was far too smart to ever whisper a word of his suspicions.

"And in any event," his editor continued, "you're not the only boots on the ground I've got. I heard that Gina insulted Becks' wife earlier in the night, didn't she? Where's *that* in the story?"

"That's not really how it played out."

His editor had smacked her forehead and made a shooing motion with her hands. "If that's how you're going to play it," she said sourly. "Off! Out! Don't send me anything else until you can work Becks into it."

Rick ground his teeth. He didn't know why he was lying about what Gina had said about Whitney, why he was omitting the potential connection to Becks. Why, for that matter, he wasn't telling his editor that he had seen the football player cowering by the stairs when the police arrived, right around when the body was found. Rick told himself it was because he wanted to investigate further, to find more information before he was forced to run a story.

"You're going to run this one though?" he had asked his editor, as he dipped out of her office. "A dollar per word?"

"Is that your standard rate with us?"

"Just about."

His editor snorted and waved him out. "For your *next* piece, about Becks, two dollars a word, if it's good."

Rick shrugged and left. He had heard those promises before. The problem was, his editor deemed nothing "good" when it finally came across her desk. The promise of a scoop was always greater than the actual facts. Truth was always a disappointment.

And now? Rick shoved his hands in his pockets and emerged out into the cool city street, breathing out plumes of white steam and trying to decide where to go next. He could try to call some old contacts in the police station, but they were traffic cops, mostly, men and women who tipped him off about DUI's sometimes when they were dealing with a particularly drunk, insensitive jerk. He could try to get an interview with Becks, but that seemed like a highway to nowhere, and Rick wasn't even certain that *Becks* understood what happened that night.

He dipped into a coffee bean roastery, one of those hipster cafés with tubes of green and brown beans that were sucked across the room above the wide-eyed patrons. What he really needed to do, Rick decided as he got in line behind a gaggle of yuppies and an old man in a three-piece suit, was run through the guest list of that night again. Think about who was there, and if there was anything, anything at all, that might make them suspicious. That might mean they had some interest, however small, in Gina Tiller's death.

Easier said than done.

As he waited, Rick felt a familiar wave of insecurity rush through him. Really, who was he to be moving through such circles? Why couldn't he just go back to the original sports beat that he had been so interested in years ago, that he had thought would be his calling, his bread and butter, his lifetime career? He thought of the 22-year-old freshly minted college graduate, with a girlfriend and a new apartment lease, who was so sure that he was on the up-and-up, who felt that a 3.9 GPA and a professor's glowing recommendation would lead him down the fast-track. Two local newspapers later, and a failed attempt at interning for a sports radio station (where Rick had been referred to—quite unoriginally—as "Nerd Boy" and pranked early and often), Rick had realized that unless he broadened his horizons, unless he lowered his vision of what "noble" kind of work he would do, he would never be able to make his rent.

The 22-year-old who had graduated—what would he think of Rick now? He'd be disappointed in the failed marriage, of course. He would probably have thought that he'd become one of those rich bachelors, moving among female sports stars and anchorwomen and models that would of course be somewhere nearby, or else the well-respected family man, with a loving and doting wife and a brood of children that loved him but never bothered him too much. That young kid hadn't experienced enough of reality to understand what a mistake the marriage had been, what a relief the divorce was—even if it left a gaping wound that Rick never seemed to fill. He would probably look with pity on the figure of Rick as he was today: thirty-four, counting dollar bills out of a crinkled wallet, trying to decide if he could splurge on a latte and if it would mean he needed to skip out on some grocery store extras later.

The truth was, Rick didn't think he was cut out for the kind of journalism that paid. He was good at it. That was why he had gotten the nicknames—*the Rat, the Mouse, the Snake*. At least the last was somewhat flattering, since it was more predatory, fierce. And since he didn't, with his close-set eyes and longer nose, resemble it like he did the other two.

But Rick also hated the way that people looked at him when they found out who he was and why he was somewhere. He hated the people who sidled up to him, whispering gossip and favors into his ears, hoping to gain a little bit of that power that he had, to influence him, to manipulate him, to *use* him. He hated the people who didn't sidle up to him, but instead looked at him as though he were the lowest vermin, as though they would prefer to be picking gum off the bottom of their shoe or prepping for a colonoscopy. Most of all, he hated the people who emailed him after he wrote a story, who somehow found a way to reach out and ask him why he had done something, why he had ruined their family, why he had no common decency at all.

Rick knew good gossip journalists. They had thick skin; they somehow better balanced the needs of the story with their responsibilities as a human being. Or at least, felt less guilty when they didn't balance them. Rick's skin was thin. He wanted people to like him. The problem was, that number had dwindled to just about zero over the years—and it wasn't looking up.

Rick ordered a honey lavender latte when he got to the front of the counter. Why not? He counted out the money recklessly, leaving a two-dollar tip. What did it matter? He was a month away from being broke. He had counted on the Becker & Miller opening party to give him fodder for half a dozen snarky articles, sold to various sites, but he found himself unable to stomach more than that single commissioned piece for *City Celebrities Daily*. He had to do something, find something, on the Gina Tiller murder. He could use the money, and then—and then, once all of that was settled, he'd find a way out. He'd do something else, be someone else.

He just needed to get the scoop first.

CHAPTER 17

"Sam!"

Sam O'Nally grinned sheepishly at Whitney. "Mind if I come in?"

Whitney blinked at him, bewildered. She looked tired today, no makeup, hair in a messy bun. Sam wished he had a wife who would look that way when she worried about him. He wouldn't mind any wife at all, really—someone to do his laundry, cook his meals, and tend to any other physical needs.

"Daniel is napping," Whitney said, still not moving away from the door. "Perhaps it's best—"

"Naw, I wanted to talk to you, actually." He took a step closer, and that seemed to do the trick. Whitney fell back, and Sam walked inside, whistling a little as he went. The place was nice—boy, was it nice!—and Sam felt a little burst of envy. He wouldn't mind a house like this. Nice street, not too close to the neighbors but not too far, two-car garage with manicured hedges out front. And the inside—"Professionally designed?" Sam said, not able to help the note of whimsy that entered his voice.

"What?" Whitney said tightly, following him as he walked towards the kitchen. "These rooms? No. I did it myself."

"Nice taste," Sam said, letting his hand rest on one of the crystal statues inside—some sort of globe suspended on a pillar. Whitney rushed towards him, fussing about, talking about balance and delicacy and the like. Sam grunted and moved forward. The house was all blue and silver and white, emphasis on the white—the granite countertops were a pale white streaked with silver, the cabinets bright white with silver handles, and the brick fireplace he could see through the open doorway—of course—a crisp white.

"What did you want to talk about?" Whitney said uneasily.

"You got anything to drink around here?"

"We have water."

Sam blushed. Some hospitality, he thought. He drummed his fingers on the countertop. He should have had a house like this, he thought. If his coaches weren't so stingy. If the team doctor hadn't suggested those three little initials, *CTE*, and then thrown up his hands defensively when Sam had confronted him.

"What?" the doctor, a weasel-faced man of forty-two, had said to him. "It might explain your alcoholism, Sam. I didn't say anything about *that.*"

Sam definitely thought he could use a drink. He looked about and pulled up a chair to the large island counter, rubbing his temples with his hands. Fine, he wasn't above asking. "You got any wine? Vodka? Something like that?" He wanted whiskey, but the others seemed more polite to ask about.

"Sam, it isn't even noon."

"Day after a party. Hungover. Hair of the dog, and all that. Aw, come on, Whit, don't look at me like that."

"I'm—I'm not," Whitney said, blushing. She rubbed her eyes. *Rough night for her, too,* Sam thought.

"Then come on. What do you have, eh? I'm not picky."

Whitney shook her head. "Water, Sam. I'm sorry. We

don't keep alcohol in the house. I might—I might have a can of soda, somewhere." When he didn't reply, she opened the fridge and dug into it, her long black skirt shimmering with her motions. Whitney had always had a nice figure, Sam thought. Tall, willowy, but solid, too, not like those stick girls that did something on social media involving posing with giant hamburgers on tropical beaches (though he did follow his fair share of such accounts).

"Here." Whitney deposited a small can in front of him. Grape soda. Sam shrugged and, to be polite, opened it and took a long sip. "Now," Whitney said, "what did you want to talk about?"

"Gina Tiller."

Whitney's eyes narrowed. "Okay."

"You know what happened with me and her, don't you?"

"That you pushed her outside a bar, yes. She fell on some broken glass, got cut up."

"Hey, I didn't put that there," Sam said, reddening. He took a deep breath, feeling a surge of something—satisfaction? embarrassment? power?—at the look of fear on Whitney's face. "Anyway, yeah. She started mocking me outside at the bar that night. Told me to go home, that I had had enough, that I needed to get my head checked before I drank any more alcohol." Sam wiped a bead of sweat off of his forehead. "Told me to come back when I didn't have Swiss cheese for brains."

"Look, I'm sorry, Sam. That's awful for her to say. But why are you telling me this? I can't do anything about it now."

Sam shook his head. "I don't *want* you to do anything. I just want to say, she was a pretty bad person, you know? I was going to sue her, actually. Defamation. She was the one who started yapping about CTE after she got up. She was bleeding from her elbows and she just started screaming at me, about how my head was messed up. Made it so that no one wanted to offer me a job—not football, obviously, I was already done with that, but you know, sports anchor jobs and such. Gina made it sound like my head was messed up, and poof! Gone."

He didn't like the look that crossed Whitney's face next. Something like pity. "But Sam," she said, "you do have it, don't you? Wasn't that one of the reasons that you retired? It's not Gina's fault that—that other people knew. I'm sure that's not why…"

"It *is* why," Sam said fiercely. He really wanted a vodka tonic. Or just some straight vodka. "And anyway, why do you care? I'm trying to help you."

Whitney stiffened. "Help me," she repeated dubiously.

"*Yes*. Look. We all know that Gina had to go, right? She wasn't a good person. She was—she was hurting everyone, all around her. It was in a lot of people's best interest for her to go."

"Sam—"

"And I know you didn't like her, either. She was talking about CTE earlier that night, wasn't she? And what she said to you on that stage…I know that must have made you pretty mad."

"Sam!"

"So I was thinking, maybe just a little money my way, that would help a lot. You know, with my lawsuit against Gina's estate. Get some justice done. Served. Whatever."

Whitney just stared at him, aghast. Her eyes seemed to be calculating everything, processing. *Good*, thought Sam. *Let her see it my way.*

"So," Whitney said slowly. "You're either blackmailing me because you think I had something to do with it and you want money to stay silent, or you're asking for payment because you killed Gina and think you deserve a little reward money for it."

Sam was silent for a few moments. "I just," he said finally, "want a little starter money. For my lawsuit. You get that, don't you?"

"Get out of my house," Whitney said. "If you try to come

back, I'm calling the police and telling them everything that you told me today."

Sam sneered at her. She was just like all the rest. He suppressed the building rage within him; all he needed to do was get Whitney to see sense, see that they were actually on the same side.

But when she picked up the phone, he rose.

"There'll be a time when you'll want my help," Sam said, pushing away the grape soda. "And good luck to you, because you won't get it."

He left, feeling Whitney's narrowed eyes following him out.

CHAPTER 18

*R*ick waited outside of Joey's Physical Therapy, a nondescript-looking warehouse on the outskirts of the city whose modesty was a tool of its discreetness: the place was a hotbed of professional athletes and recovering sports stars, catering to the elite of the elite who wanted a private, top-notch recovery program.

It was one of his old buddies who worked there that had given Rick the tip; Rick would have to pay him later, and just hope that the article made good on it. It was noon when he saw Eliza Vorne pull into the parking lot, checking the building's front door before turning into a spot. Her manicured fingers tapped on the steering wheel, and she seemed to huff as she continued to wait.

Rick got out of his car and approached. He tapped on the driver's side window.

Eliza glared at him. He could tell that she wanted to ignore him, but whatever she was guilty about got the better of her. She opened the window, eyes wary but curious.

"What do you want?" she spat.

"Morning, Eliza. Good to see you here."

"Save it, Fales. What do you want?" As she spoke, her

fingers typed quickly on the phone—probably warning whoever was inside not to come out.

"Just wanted to update you on some things I found out," Rick said, trying to keep his tone light. "I got the chance to talk to some of Gina's family members."

Eliza visibly stiffened but said nothing. She tossed her hair back and slid on a pair of giant tortoise-shell sunglasses.

"Gina's father, in particular."

"So?" Eliza snapped.

"He had a lot to say on the matter." Rick paused, giving Eliza space to fill something in. She didn't. "He's devastated, obviously."

"Not too devastated to stop him from talking to the press."

"He knows media attention will only help the community focus on the issue."

Eliza snorted. "He has money to do that. He just wants to burn everything to the ground."

"Then why'd you apply to work for him, two months ago?"

Eliza snorted. "Really? Is that what he's concerned about? His daughter dies, and he wants to know why *I* wanted to work for him a while back?"

"And then you sued him when you didn't get the job."

"I didn't," Eliza hissed. The transformation was rapid, and entire. Her whole body whipped towards Rick, and her fingers dug into the steering wheel. "I never did. You know *nothing.*"

"Eliza?"

Rick turned. Aaron Williamson stood behind him, athletic bag thrown over one shoulder. He looked from Rick to Eliza and back again, bewildered. "What's this about a lawsuit?"

"Nothing. Get in, Aaron. This guy is wasting my oxygen."

"Eliza?"

"Get in!"

Aaron cast one more suspicious glance at Rick. Then he

climbed into the passenger side of Eliza's SUV, just as Eliza's window finished rolling up. The two began talking rapidly and gesturing. Arguing, Rick thought, though he could tell Eliza was making an effort to subdue her emotions while he remained.

He stalked back to his car and watched them from there. They sat in the parking lot another three minutes, still arguing. Rick had a pit in his stomach. However all of this ended, he thought, wouldn't be good. Not for him, and not for anyone.

CHAPTER 19

*E*van paced the length of his downtown condo, trying to think.

Becks hadn't signed the papers that night. It had been Evan's stupid idea, to hold off on signing the official documents until the night of the party, making a big deal of the fact that the guests would be able to witness the legal start of the business, the moment when Becks and Evan signed on the dotted line to become official partners. It had sounded great at the time, but of course, he hadn't anticipated a murder.

Evan rubbed his temples.

Now the documents sat in his desk, unsigned and useless. If he didn't get them signed that week, his whole projected timeline for Q2 would be thrown off. But Whitney had called him that morning, telling him Becks was feeling nauseous and not up to signing the papers that day.

"Whitney. You know this is important," he had pleaded.

"It can wait a day or two."

"Whit—"

"It's not up for discussion, Evan. I have to be careful with him. You know that."

Evan had hung up, frustrated and helpless. The papers

were the only thing on his mind right then: it helped blot out other unfortunate details, like the fact that the police wanted to talk to *him* about the party, ask why he had invited Gina, ask who among the guests had a grudge against her, and blah blah blah. He had agreed to go down to the station, but the idea of it still gave him hives. The last time he had been down had been nearly ten years ago, in college, when an officer had hauled him in for trespassing and underage drinking and had him spend a night in jail, just to scare him. It had worked.

Evan bit his fingernails and continued to trudge. So much could go wrong, he thought. Perhaps it was just because he was finally on the precipice of his dreams that Evan felt sick with worry. What had happened that night had been some sort of evil omen, a harbinger of terrible events to come. Evan had never believed people when they used to joke about St. Clair's dark side, about the strangeness that could be found in its depths, but now? Now he had every reason to.

Evan picked up the phone on a whim and dialed. Becks answered on the second ring.

"Evan?"

"Hey, man," Evan said. "How you holding up?"

"I'm fine." Becks didn't sound fine—in fact, he sounded more than a little hoarse. Evan wondered how the morning had gone for him, if Becks had suffered half as much as Evan did. "You?"

"Great," Evan lied, keeping his tone light. "Crazy, huh? That'll be a memorable start to Becker & Miller."

A pause. Evan's heart skipped a beat in his chest. What if Becks felt as superstitious as he did? What if he wanted to pull the funding? Evan just needed to get those blasted papers signed.

"I wish I had just gone to business school," Becks finally said. "Then we never would have had the party."

"The business is a good idea, Becks."

"The party wasn't."

"It was. It's just—something bad happened. We had no idea, and—"

"Do you think I had something to do with it?"

"What? Becks! No, of course not. Why would you even ask me that?"

A pause. "I don't know. Never mind."

"Don't talk like that, man. Especially if the police come over, okay? What? You need a lawyer or something?"

"No." Becks sounded defeated.

"Good. Then listen. About the papers—"

"Whitney said we'd sign them Wednesday."

Little bright fireworks burst before Evan's eyes. "That's three days from now," he said, massaging his throat. "Becks, we can't delay this kind of thing."

Another pause. Evan wanted to strangle his friend through the phone. "You sure you want to go into business with me?" Becks said finally.

"Of *course* I do. Becks, come on. Stop talking like this."

Becks sighed. "I'm not feeling that well," he said. "I'm going to go."

Evan stared at his phone as Becks hung up. He resisted the urge to fling it across the room and start sobbing.

It was all so close, Evan thought. But what was he supposed to do now that it was slipping away?

CHAPTER 20

*R*ick pulled up to the Beckers' drive and shifted his
car into park. He left his hands on the steering
wheel, chewing his lower lip and thinking.

The house itself was beautiful: a broad white manor with
a stone foundation and an entryway flanked by large pillars.
The landscaping was impeccable, with rows of hedges shaped
into cones and spheres and a line of bright pink flowers
standing guard in front. Not a mansion, nothing so gaudy as
that, but a handsome home in the middle of an upscale neighborhood, walkable to downtown St. Clair.

Of course, he could imagine the reception he would get. It
had taken him long enough to find the address—a surprisingly
long time, given the celebrity status of the Beckers. They obviously valued their privacy; they would presumably have a
number of questions for him when he knocked on the door.
He felt an unfamiliar stab of guilt at what he was about to do.
Why? Surely he couldn't pity rich folks like these—especially
ones who might have had something to do with a woman's
death. Pity would cloud his judgment. It would make him
hope that something else had happened, that Evan Miller or

Sam O'Nally or Aaron Williamson or anyone else had hurt Gina Tiller—and then Rick would end up paying in the end.

The truth, as always, could be his only friend.

Rick climbed out of his car and walked up the drive to the house. He rang the buzzer and knocked on the door.

He felt quick footsteps and then the subtle change in shadows that was the peering of a face through the eyehole. The door swung open a second later, and Rick could have sworn that, for just a moment, he saw a flash of relief on Whitney's face.

"What do you want?" she said. "Sorry—I mean—who are you?"

"Rick Fales, ma'am. Good to see you again."

She ignored his hand, her face dropping. "Oh," she said. "Oh—you're the reporter, aren't you? You were there last night."

Had she been expecting the police, Rick wondered? Or perhaps the police had already been there to question her, if they hadn't the night before. "Yes, I was. I was wondering if I could ask you a few questions. About Eliza Vorne," he said, as Whitney stepped back from the door and sighed, beginning to shut it.

At the mention of her friend's name, Whitney hesitated, and Rick began talking rapidly. "I understand that she applied for a job working under Mr. Tiller a few months ago—Gina's father. And then she pursued legal action against him when she did not get it—"

"She didn't," Whitney said darkly.

"Well, I'd love to have you clear that up for me. Maybe I've been misinformed. But it's an odd grudge to have, given the circumstances—"

"Rick, is it? Please. I'm exhausted. My husband is exhausted. There's nothing I can possibly say to you, nor anything that I think I should. A woman was murdered. I have no comment for the papers." She gave him a look of disdain mixed with pity, and Rick recoiled. Pity was always the worst.

Whitney shut the door.

Rick blinked, trying to recover. He could knock on the door again, try another angle. Perhaps state even wilder rumors about Eliza and see if Whitney bit. Perhaps insinuate things about her husband and see if she started defending him, or if she grew afraid.

In the end, though, the look of pity kept him back. He needed to go home and recuperate—have a drink, regroup, try to wash some of that disgusting pity from his pores. He would be on his game these next few days, no matter what he had to do. He would deliver the story that he needed to and move on. As soon as he got his head on straight.

Rick was almost back to his car when a voice called out to him. Rick blinked, shocked. The tall, broad-shouldered figure of Daniel Becker approached him in loping strides.

"Can I ride with you?" Becks said, slipping into the passenger side without waiting for a response.

"Your wife okay with this?" Rick asked, still bewildered. But he climbed into the car and dutifully started it.

"She's on the phone. She'll be a while." Becks shot Rick a quick smile. "Stop panicking. Didn't you come to talk to me?"

Rick hid his surprise by a dutiful focus on backing out of the drive. When he was on the road, he said, "I take it you're feeling better today."

Becks shrugged, embarrassed. He leaned his forehead against his window. "A bit nauseous this morning, but yeah. Good today."

"Glad to hear it."

An awkward silence fell over the car. *Daniel Becker!* Rick thought. He had *Daniel Becker* in his car!

"Did you hear what I said to her?" Rick blurted, a few seconds later. "To your wife, I mean."

"About Eliza?" Becks shrugged. "Not sure why you care. Eliza didn't do anything to Gina."

"Does that mean you know who did?"

"No. Do you?"

Rick considered bluffing, but ended up shaking his head. "But you have to admit," he said, "it looks suspicious—the lawsuit."

"But Eliza didn't sue Lyle Tiller," Becks said. "That's what I wanted to tell you."

Rick glanced over at Becks, intrigued. "That's why you gave your wife the slip and wanted to talk to some lowly gossip reporter like me?"

Becks shrugged sheepishly. "I don't know who you write for. You seemed fine last night. I just—well, Eliza's a friend. If Whitney doesn't want to tell you, I will. Lyle Tiller was harassing Eliza."

Rick tried not to let the doubt show plainly on his face. He knew CTE didn't cause outright delusions, at least, not that he knew of, but how far could he trust Becks' words? His interpretations? "Harassing, like…?"

"He knew Eliza was interested in working for him. So he dangled a job offer in front of her, but told her she'd have to go through the formal interview process. Kept setting up interviews privately with him at his office. On the second or third one he made a move on her, and then tried to grab her by the wrist when she left."

"How do you know this?"

"She told Whitney. In front of me."

"And you believe her?"

Becks snorted. "Yes. Entirely."

"But the lawsuit…"

"There *was* no lawsuit. She threatened one, yeah, just to get him to stop trying to contact her after that. Obviously she wasn't going to take any job. Lyle didn't really take kindly to all of that. He threatened to have Wills pulled off the team if she tried to do anything like that."

"Wills?"

"Aaron Williamson. They were dating at the time."

"How long ago was that?"

Becks shrugged. "A month? Longer, maybe—a couple of months or so. I don't know."

Rick was quiet, calculating. If that was true, then Eliza still had every reason to dislike Gina Tiller—though in any of these scenarios, it was hard to understand why, exactly, she would have a motivation to kill her. To get back at the father? That seemed a bit dramatic.

"Did Eliza have any other personal feelings towards Gina?" Rick asked.

Becks frowned. "This is all—what is it, deep background? Off the record? I don't want to be quoted in any articles."

"You won't be," Rick assured him, not mentioning that it was mostly because Daniel Becker would not be considered a reliable source. Not now.

"Well, the answer is no, anyway. I don't know—I don't think most people like Gina, from what Whit tells me. Why? Why do you think Eliza had something to do with it?"

"Why is Aaron Williamson getting physical therapy?" Rick said, changing the subject. "I saw him leaving a center this morning."

Becks blinked, then shrugged. "I wouldn't know," he said, unable to keep the bitter note from his voice. "I don't really keep up with that kind of stuff anymore."

They rode in silence for some time. Rick was doing a large loop around St. Clair, figuring Becks had a good twenty or thirty minutes at least before Whitney noticed he was missing. His mind kept whirring, trying to make sense of everything. He wanted to ask more about what Becks remembered that night, if anything had come back to him, but he couldn't seem to find a way to broach the subject—not without sounding accusatory.

"You seem cheerful this morning," Rick said finally.

"I'm okay."

Maybe relieved to have Gina Tiller out of the way, Rick thought darkly, and shoved the thought away. No. Of course that couldn't be true. The man sitting in his passenger seat, looking down at his large hands, brow furrowed in intense thought—that man surely wasn't a murderer.

"Are you feeling nauseous?" Rick said nervously, noticing how still Becks had gone.

"No. Not anymore. I'm fine." Becks shook himself and straightened. "Whitney called the doctors, of course. She wanted to bring me in. They told her it was probably stress and told me to drink some ginger ale." He laughed humorlessly. "They were right, though. That seemed to have done the trick."

He's lonely, Rick realized, feeling another unwelcome wave of sympathy for the ex-footballer. His football friends probably rarely talked to him anymore, he had had an ugly and public falling-out with his family years ago, and his wife was probably more concerned with talking CTE symptoms and health details than actually having a human, normal conversation. Becks didn't run out because he wanted to correct a point about Eliza. He ran out because he was desperate for some, for any, relief. For a human interaction that approximated normal.

Slowly, Rick pulled back on the street that led to Becks' house. He felt Becks noticeably stiffen as they did so.

"Did you want to tell me anything else?" Rick finally ventured. "Anything before I drop you back off?"

"About what?"

It was like dealing with a child. "About last night. At the mansion. About Gina's death."

"Eliza didn't do anything."

"Mmhmm. I know, you told me as much. What about who did do it—anything you remember there?"

Becks looked sideways at him. "You're asking me if I remember doing anything to her."

"Well—yes. I guess so. Do you?"

"No."

"Okay."

"But you still think that maybe I did."

Rick held up one hand in a *who knows* gesture. "You ever have gaps in your memory like that? Would be pretty odd, if you weren't drinking."

Becks was silent, stewing. *That's a yes,* Rick thought.

"Well," Rick said, loudly, too cheerfully, as he pulled back into Becks' drive. "It could have been anyone, really. I don't mean to make you think that I just suspect you. It's a puzzle, that's all. A puzzle to figure out."

"Will you tell me? When you do figure it out?" Becks question was fervent and earnest as Rick killed his engine. The reporter glanced over at Becks, who was looking at him with a wide-eyed and hopeful expression. Rick felt suddenly uneasily. "You're going to keep looking into what happened to Gina?"

"Yes," Rick said slowly. "I'm going to keep looking."

"You'll keep me in the loop?"

"I mean—yes, sure I will. I'll give you my card, too? And that way, if you remember anything, you can get in touch with me."

Becks shrugged, but took the card when Rick offered it to him. "I really hope you figure out what happened," Becks mumbled, turning the card over in his massive fingers. "I really hope you do."

And then he was out of the car and loping back towards his house.

CHAPTER 21

$\mathcal{M}$onday morning dawned; Becks woke up feeling light and clearheaded, until he thought again of Gina, of the police, of his wild decision to run out and talk to the reporter. What had been the point of that? *Perhaps CTE affects decision-making*, that snake-like voice in his head whispered, and Becks pushed it away as he tossed off the rest of his covers.

He made himself coffee and found a note in the kitchen from Whitney, telling him that she was running to the pharmacy and that she had left the cereal out on the counter for him. Becks felt a stab of resentment at the thought that perhaps Whitney felt he was just like a child, too much of a burden to take anywhere anymore. But he quickly suppressed it.

The details of the day before played back to him, strong and distinct. He had run after Fales, and why? He had been worried that Fales would think poorly of Eliza, that Whitney's refusal to correct the reporter's false information would lead to a scandalous story with no basis in truth. But really, was that true? Or had Becks known that such threats were part of the journalist's currency? Had Becks gone out there, in actuality, just because he was so desperate for someone else to think well of him? Because he wanted to manipulate the reporter, get him to like him?

Because he was afraid, and didn't quite trust himself?

Becks shook his head and took his cereal over to the couch. He couldn't think like that. Wouldn't, now that he had some space and time to think.

He flipped through the channels and dug out the newspaper from recycling. He didn't read much anymore—it tended to give him a headache—so Whitney had taken to trashing the papers after she read them. When he finally snapped the paper open, he wished he hadn't: the death of Gina Tiller had made the front page, with the headline "Popular Socialite Found Dead at Disgraced Footballer's Party." The article itself seemed to imply that Gina Tiller had had too much to drink and had toppled off the balcony: the author did away with Gina's murder in the first few paragraphs, before moving almost entirely to focus on Daniel Becker's health and professional troubles, including a quote from the Gryphons' former team doctor, a recounting of the infamous tackle, and a short blurb on Becks' new company that "was formed together with one of Becker's high school friends."

Becks dialed Evan.

"Becks!" Evan said. "Was just thinking of giving you a call. How goes it?"

"We got some publicity."

"How's that?"

"The paper."

"Local or national?"

"National."

A pause as Evan digested this and swallowed. "Well," Evan said, still trying to sound cheery, "I haven't seen that one yet. Hold on." Becks heard typing on the other end of the line. "Ah. Well. It's ah—it's to be expected, isn't it?"

Evan was doing a poor job of hiding his nervousness. "At least they're not implying here that I killed her," Becks said sourly. "At least not in so many words. I'm sure that will come later, though, won't it?"

"No, of course not," Evan said unconvincingly. "You didn't, so why would they? Never mind the papers. Dying business. They're all just trying to keep circulation up." It was the same thing that Evan had said to Becks when the first scandal hit, when Whitney and Evan had spent weeks trying to shield Becks from the worst of it.

"I'm sorry."

"Don't be sorry."

"I ruined the launch. If I hadn't been there—"

"Then what? Gina still would have taken a spill off the balcony. Don't talk that way, okay, Becks?"

Becks was silent.

"Becks? Becks, you know I don't think you had anything to do with this, right?"

"Yeah. Look. I'm a bit tired. I'm going to go."

"Sure. See you Wednesday? To sign the papers? Or sooner, honestly, if you have time for it."

Becks had entirely forgotten about that part. He hadn't signed them Saturday? The night was still a blur in his head. Becks' stomach clenched. "Yeah, Wednesday," he said. "Sure. Right."

He hung up and walked back over to the couch. His phone was buzzing with new text messages and phone calls—probably reporters and other bloodsuckers whom he had blocked on different lines. He picked up the phone and scrolled through a few, looking for the familiar greeting that would send ice down his spine. *Danny darling*, his mother would always begin. *Danny darling, how are you? Danny darling, it's been too long.*

Only Whitney knew the full extent of that betrayal there; he had hidden the details even from Evan, had been too ashamed to explain to his accountant why nearly a million dollars had gone missing from his bank account. "I moved it to another account—a spending account," he had told the accountant lamely. "It didn't last long." He had suffered through the man's disapproval and gentle chastisement, had sold an investment property (back when he was still trying to do such things) off in Florida to ensure he had enough cash that month to pay all of his bills.

"It's kind of their money too," he had even told Whitney, because he had been so desperate not to see the theft for what it really was, for what it meant for his relationship with his family. "My mom drove me to football practice every day when I was a kid. She had two jobs—"

"That's what every parent is supposed to do," Whitney fired back. "Not forge their kid's signature on a bunch of checks."

Becks had wanted to talk about the missing money with his mother; Whitney had told him not to bother, that they would simply heighten their security and discreetly warn the bank of potential fraud. "It will make it at least so you can go home for Christmas," Whitney said, in a disgusted tone that made it clear she did not plan to go with him. To her credit, though, she never said a word against Becks' family, only bottled her hatred for them up, so much so that Becks could feel it steaming out of her ears whenever he mentioned them.

In the end, of course, he had called his brother, thinking he could broach the topic carefully with his sole sibling. For a while, Joseph Becker had been a head taller and a good deal stronger than Becks, his younger brother, but high school had done away with the advantage, and as Becks became bigger, he also became richer and more successful. Joseph had dealt with the change good-naturedly; he had always had a quick tongue and an easier manner, and for some time came to all of Becks' football games, mother in tow. Only later, once Becks married Whitney and bought his own house in St. Clair, a "bougie neighborhood," as Joseph said, did the relationship between them become tense. Their mother grew sick, some sort of undiagnosed blood disease, and though Becks footed all the medical bills he never visited often enough to satisfy either one of them. They felt his excuses about football practice to be selfish and narrow-minded; sometimes, he believed them.

"Fame has changed you," Joseph had said. They fought, they made up. Things had been going well, up until Whitney had audited their bank statements.

"Little Danny," Joseph had said, when he had answered the phone that day. "What can I do you for?"

"I'm missing money in my accounts," Becks blurted. He was so desperate to have Joseph contradict him, to laugh at him and tell him he had it all wrong, to explain it all away.

But instead his brother grew silent. "That's a hello for you," he finally said. "I suppose you're going to say next that you think *I* took it."

"No," Becks lied. "I was wondering—maybe Mom talked to you about it?"

"About stealing from you?"

"No, I—"

"How do we know where your money went?" Joseph said sourly. "You don't think you moved something around? Bought a new property? Maybe your financial advisor invested it. You know better than I do why rich people's money gets shuffled places."

"I don't—"

"I offered to help you out before, Danny. Not my fault if you're being irresponsible with it."

"I'm not," Becks said hotly. "I'm missing a million dollars.

The bank said I wrote checks and wired money to a new account at *your and Mom's* bank. The money was moved offshore, and the account is closed now. You want to tell me what that is about?"

"It's all about money to you, isn't it?" Joseph had snarled, not missing a beat. "Jeez. I should have known when you called. Anything else you want to accuse me of? Sleeping with your wife? Sabotaging your career? Sorry Danny, but it's about time to tell you: I'm not responsible for everything going wrong in your life." He slammed down the phone.

Becks called his mother next, who didn't pick up. In the next few days, she would call him, a dozen, two dozen times, leaving voicemails that ranged from angry to pleading, telling him that he had gotten it all wrong, that Joseph had told her about "Danny's nasty accusations," reminding him that she had never asked him for a dime, never, even when he got that ten-million dollar contract the other year, as if somehow that had any bearing on whether she could steal from him. In the end, Becks had almost called her back—until he played the last message, a reckless, desperate one, where his mother had told him that she knew Whitney would never let him "help out the family," so she had taken matters into her own hands, and she knew he wouldn't begrudge her that, would he? Not her darling boy.

Disgusted and rent, Becks had deleted all of the messages.

When he had suffered the biggest disgrace of his career, Joseph and his mother had been silent. When he had officially retired from football, they said nothing. Only when news got out that he was planning to start something new did their feelers begin, probing him from new numbers, telling him that they were willing to forgive his accusations, that they wanted to reconcile. Sometimes, on dark days, he wanted to. What was a little money when it came to blood? But then he would think to himself that they saw him only as vulnerable and weak, a mark to get a little more money out of before the crazy Daniel Becker ran dry, and died exiled and ruined.

Becks shut off his phone and lay down on the couch. He was tired now; depression closed in upon him again, dark and smothering. All that he wanted to do was sleep, sleep and have the last year of his life be lifted away.

CHAPTER 22

$\mathcal{R}$ick pulled up to the security gate at the St. Clair Yacht Club, where a middle-aged, stout woman in a polo and white slacks peered dubiously out at his rusted sedan.

"Yes?" she said, voice tight with suspicion. Rick blushed. He didn't *want* to care that this wealthy suburbanite thought poorly of him.

"I have a meeting here. With Mr. Lyle Tiller."

The woman only stared at him. Rick smiled, which seemed ridiculous; the woman's eyes only narrowed further, and without taking her eyes off of him, she picked up the gray phone and dialed a three-digit number. Rick was only sure it was not 9-1-1 when she said, "Yes, a man here to see Mr. Tiller. No, he didn't identify himself."

"You didn't ask!" Rick called.

"Sorry, repeat that. Yes. Okay. Well...all right, then." Reluctantly, the woman hung up the phone. "What's your name?" she barked at Rick.

"Rick Fales."

"I'll need some I.D."

"Sorry, forgot it."

"Then I apologize, I can't let you in."

"I'm not sure Mr. Tiller will be pleased about that."

The woman scowled. Rick considered making a show of finding his I.D. and handing it to her—he had it snugly in his back pocket, as he always did—but he wanted to wield whatever petty power he had to annoy her, in recompense for her snobbery. *It's the little things in life*, he thought.

"Hold on," the woman said sourly. "I'll look you up. Spell 'Fails'?"

*F-u-c...*Rick thought. But he spelled it, and the woman spent a few moments tapping into her phone and then looking from its screen to Rick's face dubiously.

"You've lost some weight," she said accusingly.

"Cardio." In fact, Rick had just been happier when the most searchable photo of him was taken—newly engaged, young and eager, not yet beaten down by the world. That blasted picture was always the one that showed up when he searched himself, as if to mock him with the memory of all of his false hopes.

The woman buzzed him in without another word, eyes sliding away from him as if he was no longer worth her time.

"Thank you!" Rick shouted, loud and overly cheery, and drove through noisily, gunning his car just to get past the gate and before the self-proclaimed elites of society could change their minds. He parked in the long, thin lot to the right, ignoring looks from housewives and househusbands and retirees and everyone else who'd be at the club midday on a Monday, stalking up the long walk to the yacht club's front doors.

He was greeted by a young woman in a pencil skirt and pink blouse who ushered him up to a meeting room, a private place with a lakefront view that was empty of all except a few bookcases and an oversized oak desk. Rick wandered to the window and watched the icy, churning lake for a few minutes, wondering if this had all been some elaborate plan to trap him, if prestigious yacht clubs could also be the scenes of movie-like assassinations and body disposals for their rich patrons. He even went to the door and tried the lock, and was not a little disappointed to find that it opened easily, and that he was not, in fact, a prisoner.

A few minutes later, the door opened and the young woman reappeared, preceding Lyle Tiller into the room.

The Gryphons' owner was shorter than Rick had antici-pated, since Rick had fallen victim to that persistent fallacy that people seen on TV *must* be larger than life. Lyle Tiller was wide enough, though, with an oversized head and a mane of gray-white curls, with a barrel-sized chest ready to burst out of the thin button-down shirt that he had wrestled on. Rick had only time to notice the plethora of rings on the football team owner's thick, square fingers before Lyle Tiller barked, "That's all, Chelsea! Leave us," startling Rick to attention.

"Here," Lyle said, pointing to the two small chairs facing the lake. Rick thought it surprisingly egalitarian for the old man, whom he had assumed would want to sit behind some oversized desk where he could look down on the lower-class reporter. "I'm glad we could meet in person finally. Easier to talk about more...sensitive matters," Lyle continued gruffly.

"Yes." Rick almost added a "sir" and decided against it. Best not to come off as too much of a sycophant.

"Did you see who murdered my baby?"

Lyle did not look at Rick as the question was posed; he kept his gaze steadfastly fixed on the water, and Rick took the opportunity to assess the man's expression. Distant, reserved. No naked raw pain or grief. But then, a man of his status would know how to maintain a poker face.

"I didn't see it," Rick said. "I'm sorry."

Lyle grunted in what could have been acknowledgment or dismissal. "Tell me what you did see."

Smart, thought Rick. First, Lyle Tiller had gotten his attention by waving information about Eliza Vorne in his face.

Then, he had invited Rick over to talk in person, to discuss "more sensitive" topics. And he was going to use this time to try to squeeze all the details from Rick that he could, to find out from someone at the party what had gone down. Rick guessed that no other attendees would be chomping at the bit to meet with Lyle Tiller, under the circumstances.

"It's not much," Rick warned. But he dutifully launched into an account of arriving that night, of Gina interrupting Evan's speech, of hearing the wail of sirens not long after. He left out many details—including finding Becks in the staircase —and finished when the police had pulled him aside to ask a few questions.

Lyle Tiller was staring at him now, gray, fish-like eyes intent upon him. "And?" he said finally.

"And that's it."

"Where was Evan Miller? When Gina was murdered."

Rick swallowed. Was it definitely murder, then? Couldn't it have been what some people had speculated that night—a drunk woman falling off a balcony after too much to drink? Rick wouldn't try posing the possibility to Lyle, though.

"I don't know where Evan was," Rick said carefully. "Mingling with everyone, I think. Trolling for donors and such."

Lyle's lip curled. "He wanted me at that damn party," he said. "Thought I would come and open my checkbook for him. You know what his friend cost me? The bad publicity? All because he dropped his blasted shoulder in that tackle." The rage seemed to enliven him, and he straightened in his chair. "I told him to get lost and never contact me again. I told Gina not to go. Gina's heart is too soft. She always wants to see the good in people."

Sure, Rick thought. The image did not jive with his memory of Gina Tiller that night.

"That Miller kid did this," Lyle continued. "I know he did. He killed my baby girl."

"How do you know?"

"I know. That boy has secrets. Good for nothing. Probably was in love with Gina and she rejected him or something."

Rick tried to hide his disappointment. The idea that the murderer—if indeed there was one—was someone other than Becks filled him with hope. He wasn't proud of it, but there it was: Rick didn't want Daniel Becker to be the bad guy. Probably some warped process of projecting his own insecurities on the fallen football star, of sympathizing with the golden boy now shunned by society. Except, Rick Fales had never been a golden boy, not even for a little.

"I don't think Evan was in love with her," Rick said, gently as he could. He couldn't be certain, of course, but he didn't see any of that sort of tension at the party.

"Nonsense. Everyone is."

"Do you have any other reasons for thinking Evan had something to do with this?"

Lyle sneered again. "You going to put this in your paper? 'Victim's father accuses Evan Miller of murder'?"

"No. It wouldn't be worth the headache. Now if you have a piece of evidence implicating him…I could run with that. More than just an accusation from a mourning father."

Lyle didn't take offense to this. He looked back out at the lake, his eyes cold and calculating.

"Gina is friendly with a lawyer out in the city," Lyle said, still struggling to speak about his daughter in the past tense. "Business lawyer. He told her something privileged—Evan is one of his clients."

Rick's stomach fluttered. For a moment he wished that he too could be a rich, young socialite, for whom secrets would be easy to collect and cajole out of people. "Okay," Rick said, when Lyle paused.

"You can't run this. He could be disbarred. You'll have to confirm this another way."

"Okay."

Lyle nodded, still not meeting Rick's eyes. "Becker &

Miller, the business? The one that the party was for? Well, Evan Miller planned to move the whole thing to Florida in the next six months. That's what he wanted the lawyer's help for. He hooked him up with an attorney in Florida, and they were already working on the papers to move it down there."

"Did the Beckers know?"

Lyle looked at Rick scathingly. "What do you think? He had it in the contract that he had full legal right to move the business. Fine print. I don't think Becks' head is good enough to really see that, do you? Evan Miller probably figured he'd pull one over on the guy."

A chill ran through Rick. Lyle looked almost proud.

"That was my Gina," he said, shaking his head. "Too smart for her own good. Knew all sorts of things about all sorts of people. She always got it out of them."

"It's dangerous, keeping that many secrets."

Lyle's face hardened. "You send me the article when it's done," he said brusquely, rising. "I want to see that boy burn."

CHAPTER 23

*E*liza scrolled through her phone at the neighborhood wine bar, rubbing the back of her calf with her toe.

She should never have gotten involved; that much was obvious. But she couldn't leave Aaron in the lurch, not after everything they'd been through. And she knew how close he was to those sponsorships, how he just needed to make it through a few more weeks. It wasn't fair that one idiotic weekend could ruin someone's career.

Oh, she had berated him enough about it, to be sure. *Skiing?* she had cried. *What girl convinced you that that was a good idea?*

It wasn't a girl, it turned out—it was some of Aaron's high school friends, who thought a trip up to Whistler for a pro-football player was a fantastic plan. And Aaron, who always seemed insecure to Eliza about how much his high school friends still liked him (as if they wouldn't, as if they'd give up the opportunity to brush shoulders with their most successful friend), had agreed to go, and what's more, had agreed to ski.

It could have been worse, of course—a strained wrist, Aaron had said, though she had some inkling that it might be worse, that Aaron could be covering up some sort of hairline

fracture. He had to make it through two more weeks of practice before his sponsorship deals closed. Then he could take
time off—and only then. If he needed to.

"Eliza!"

Eliza jumped before recovering herself. "Whitney," she
said, embracing her friend. They squeezed hands and
Whitney eased herself onto the stool next to her. "How are
you? How is everything?"

Whitney smiled faintly at her. Whitney the soldier, the stal-
wart, the supporter. Eliza could only imagine what she had
been going through this past year.

"I'm fine," Whitney said. "How are you holding up?"

Eliza dismissed the question with a wave of her hand.
"Good, as always. How's Becks?"

"He's doing well." Whitney gave her another bland smile,
and Eliza suppressed a shudder. When she had met Whitney,
back in junior year, Whitney already had a promise ring from
Becks and spoke about her future as though it would depend
solely on Becks' football career. Eliza remembered thinking
that first, Whitney was nuts, next, that she was lucky (once she
met Becks and saw how he treated her), and third, that only
someone like Whitney could flourish in that kind of relationship. Whitney was organized, disciplined, and matter-of-fact:
she helped organize Becks' life and was his emotional support
when things went wrong. In fact, Whitney and Becks spent so
much of their free time together that Eliza would bet she
never would have actually become friends with Whitney, had
they not been assigned to work on junior project together,
something that necessitated weekly library meet-ups and a few
Friday night box-wine-fueled brainstorming sessions as well.

Now? Now Whitney was still organized, disciplined, and
matter-of-fact: her focus was just different. Eliza knew the
rumors. Eliza knew that *Whitney* knew the rumors. Still,
Whitney went through the motions, played the part, deflected
any and all suggestions that there might be something wrong

with Becks—even if all of them could tell how off he had been acting at the party, how much he had deteriorated over the past few months. Whitney looked exactly like herself, except more strained, as if the skin stretched over her bones had begun to tighten and thin, as if her smile were one millimeter away from breaking.

Whitney ordered a cocktail, and Eliza indicated that she would have the same. Eliza didn't know the reason for the distance between them: she could only assume it had to do with Whitney's desire to keep Becks safe, but it hurt none-theless. Eliza could keep a secret. She *would* keep it.

"Listen, I wanted to ask you," Whitney said, as their azure drinks were deposited before them in martini glasses. "Sam O'Nally. How much do you know about him?"

Eliza snorted. "Washed up football player. Not like Becks," Eliza rushed to correct. "I just mean, he's been retired for a few years now. Raging alcoholic. Some people say CTE too, but I don't know. I suppose it presents differently in everyone."

Whitney shifted uncomfortably but did not respond.

"Why?" Eliza pressed. "Has Becks been talking to him?"

"No. He came over yesterday and wanted to talk to me."

"Sam did?"

"Yes."

Eliza frowned. "That's funny, because he's been calling and trying to meet with *me*."

For some reason, Whitney looked almost relieved at this fact. "Well, I don't feel so targeted then," she said, with a short laugh. "What does he want with you?"

"Don't know. I haven't picked up. What did he say to you?"

Whitney frowned. "It was nonsensical. He basically wanted money, I think. He was kind of threatening us."

"Threatening you?"

"Yes. Implying Becks had something to do with it. That if we'd pay him, he'd keep quiet about it."

"Moron!"

"I agree," Whitney said, taking another sip of her drink. "Anyway, I told him to get lost. You'll have to tell me if that's what he wants from you, too."

Eliza shook her head. She had been friendly with Sam only briefly, when she had first been dating Aaron, because Aaron was friendly with everyone. Even then it didn't take her long to see that there was an uncomfortable edge to the man, which only seemed to worsen after his retirement. She had figured he had something to say to her about Becks—whether because Becks actually had something to do with what happened to Gina that night, or because Sam wanted to tell her that Becks did.

Either way, Eliza wasn't chomping at the bit to speak to him.

"I'll handle Sam," Eliza said. "Don't worry about him."

"I'm not," Whitney said, tensing. "Sorry—I mean, we're fine. We're dealing with things. Have the police talked to you yet?"

"No. You?"

"No. Did you—did you see anything that night?"

Eliza felt a wave of pity for the woman. Suspecting what everyone else did, even if they were smart enough not to say it yet. Gina Tiller could have tumbled off the balcony, sure. Or she could have been killed by any one of the dozens of people who probably disliked her. But even Whitney seemed to believe that the truth lay closer to home. That Daniel Becker, the beloved golden boy, had finally finished his downward spiral.

"I didn't see anything," Eliza said. "You were with Becks, I'm guessing?"

"Most of the night," Whitney said stiffly.

Eliza reached over and squeezed her hand. "It will be all right, Whit. I'll come visit. I'll even bring Aaron, if you think it would cheer him up."

"Thanks. That's kind of you, but—he's fine. No need for visitors."

"Let us come over. We'll cook for you, or order pizza. I'm sure Becks wouldn't mind the company, after—"

"No."

Eliza drew back at the force of the word, suppressing a shudder.

CHAPTER 24

*S*am paced back and forth in the apartment building's lobby. He could see the security guard eyeing him, deciding if he wanted to make trouble with the six-five bear of a man trodding on the place's red-striped carpets. *Try me*, Sam thought, fists clenching. *Just try me.*

The clock struck seven as he completed his fifth lap. Eliza couldn't have been at work this long—she was a socialite, for goodness sake, the kind who had a media job at some fancy television station just for some cocktail conversation, not the kind to stay late and work hard at anything because daddy's money would always be a soft cushion.

Night and day from the world Sam O'Nally grew up in.

Finally, five after seven, the door to the apartment complex swung open. Sam saw the refracted light from a hundred rain-drops on the door, then the figure of Eliza emerging from the darkness, swinging shut her umbrella and pulling her raincoat more tightly about her. Sam had only a moment to think how warm the March evening must have been for rain before Eliza caught sight of him and blanched.

He cut across the room to her; Eliza swung sideways and made for the elevators. Sam felt the security guard stiffen and saw his hand go to his pocket (for a cell phone, the guards never carried), and then Sam was in front of Eliza, a grin spreading across his face that he meant to be friendly.

"Got my messages, I suppose?" he said.

"Sir, if you could——"

"Told you I was here to see her," Sam said, jerking one thumb at Eliza. Eliza, to her credit, seemed to recover, straightening her shoulders and holding her umbrella in front of her feet like a walking stick. "Isn't that right, Eliza?"

"You didn't warn me you were showing up here, Sam."

The security guard shifted his weight nervously. "Sir, if you could just——"

"We'll talk in the lobby," Eliza said coldly. She ignored the security guard. "Come on. There's a couch in the center."

"I'd rather talk in private."

"I didn't invite you, Sam. You're not coming up to my place."

Sam followed her back out into the lobby. "Do you want me to...?" The security guard trailed off, then shrugged his shoulders, embarrassed, and retreated back to his stand. Sam gave him a hearty wave.

They positioned themselves on the circular red couch in the center, benches snaking around a giant tree in the middle of the complex, kept alive either by the glass ceiling of the place (currently pattering with raindrops), by magic, or by some combination of the two. Sam bet a tree like that could live in St. Clair, glass ceiling or no. Things grew in unexpected places in that town. He shuddered.

"Go on, Sam," Eliza said curtly. "You know you shouldn't be showing up unannounced to women's homes."

"I wouldn't have to do anything unannounced if you had just texted me back."

Eliza shrugged.

Sam picked a hair off of his jeans, trying to think where to begin. He wanted money; of course he wanted money. Eliza had money. But she wouldn't give it to him. That was one thing he learned about all of these rich folks: they always felt more entitled to money than you, no matter how much extra they had. He had once been walking with the son of a millionaire whose father had made a number of generous donations to the football team. Together they had spotted a twenty-dollar bill on the ground. "Right on!" the twenty-one-year-old heir had shouted, snatching up the bill and pocketing it. Meanwhile, Sam hadn't even gotten a contract yet and had been living in a squat apartment with the heat turned off to save money.

"I'm wondering," Sam said carefully to Eliza, "what you saw at the party."

Eliza frowned at him. "That's vague, Sam."

"You know what I mean."

"You want to know if I saw who killed Gina."

Sam shrugged. "In that arena, sure."

"And I suppose you're implying that you have information on that."

She was so smug. So sure of herself. Sam wanted to say a few things right there that would knock her off her pedestal. Things that would rock her world.

"I might know something," Sam said, shrugging. "Doesn't mean I'm going to say anything."

"I'm not giving you any money."

Sam flushed. "I wasn't *asking* you to."

"Then why did you want to meet?"

Sam couldn't answer. He felt humiliated; a quick twist of his head showed him that two people were just a few feet away on the couch, heads bent together over a book, possibly listening in and pretending to read. He hadn't come to ask the stupid woman for money. Of course he hadn't—not like that, at least. Why had she said that?

"Do you remember that night?" Eliza pressed. "Aaron told me that sometimes you black out. At parties. You were drunk, weren't you? Do you think anything you say to the police will hold weight?"

Sam flushed further. His hands began to shake. A horrible thought entered his head: *what if she knew already?* What if she was in on it? Sam didn't know all the details…he had seen something…he had thought…and what did Eliza have on him?

"I'm not trying to be mean," Eliza said. "But look at it this way, Sam. You have a history of assault. And I'm not counting that incident with Gina. Two men, separate occasions, when you were drinking."

"One of those charges was dropped," Sam said hotly.

"Probation for the other, was it? And you've also had, what, three failed lawsuits in the past two years? You need money. You have a history of aggression and drinking. I'm saying this as your friend, Sam. Let it go. Don't go around making threats—I'm not saying you are, I'm saying that's what it looks like. It will be better for you in the long run."

"You don't know what's good for me," Sam said. The words were like lava in his mouth. He was having trouble thinking and pressed the heels of his hands against his temples. Eliza stiffened and drew back. "You don't know why I came to talk to you."

"All right. Then why did you?"

"Doesn't matter now," Sam hissed. "Never mind. I knew you wouldn't help me."

Eliza blinked. She opened her mouth, thought better of it, and sighed.

"You think you're better than me," Sam spat. "I know you do. But I'm not the only one who's made some mistakes, you know. That's what everyone forgets. That they're not perfect, either."

"I never said—"

"And at least I protect my friends," Sam continued. He wanted to shout the words, wanted to see Eliza's face crumple and dissolve into tears, wanted her to feel at least a portion of the hurt that he did. "I don't go running my mouth about their business. Especially not to people who can hurt them."

Eliza went still. "You don't know what you're talking about."

"Oh, I do. What would your friends think if they knew? What would Aaron say?"

Eliza stood abruptly. "I don't need to sit here and listen to this," she said, but her voice was pinched, and she looked nervous. "Get out of here, and don't try to see me again."

Sam watched her stride towards the elevators, head high, not deigning to look back. *That's fine,* Sam thought. *It will catch up with you at some point, and then...*

It wouldn't solve any of Sam's problems, of course, but if he had to go down, he wanted to take everyone down with him.

CHAPTER 25

"**Y**ou seem a little nervous," Aaron said as Eliza drove down the highway, jabbing at radio stations with her right hand. "You sure you want to do this?"

"We have to visit him," Eliza said, finally clucking with annoyance and shutting the radio off. "He needs us. Whitney too."

"I agree. But I could go alone, if you want."

"Why would I want that?"

"I don't know. You seem jittery."

"I'm *not*," Eliza said, and sucked in a deep breath. "Anyway. We're going, so that's that. Tell me how physical therapy is coming along."

"Went this morning, feeling fine," Aaron lied. He *had* gone this morning, but his wrist had been throbbing with pain the whole while. "Nothing but rest is going to help that," the trainer had warned, but Aaron had refused to accept it. Just a few more weeks, and he could take the rest that he needed. Not until then.

"Do you think anyone else knows? About your wrist?"

"No, of course not. Why would they?"

Eliza shrugged.

"Eliza. Why would they?"

She made a face. "How should I know, Aaron? Maybe that reporter is talking. Maybe people inside the place are talking. You're not exactly low profile, you know."

Aaron felt the familiar churn in his stomach whenever he let his thoughts drift this way. But no. For his own sanity, he wouldn't believe it. It would have to be okay.

They drove the rest of the way in silence, Eliza deep in her thoughts, Aaron alone with his. He wondered if Eliza knew more than she was letting on, if she was angry with him for something else, something he had done his very best to hide...

When they pulled up to the Beckers' house, Eliza parallel parked in three easy, clean motions. They walked up to the front door and knocked.

"She might not answer," Eliza said, biting her thumbnail. "She doesn't want any visitors, I think."

Aaron reached over her and knocked again, loudly.

Seconds later, the door swung open. Becks stood in the threshold.

A wide grin split his face when he saw them, and Aaron felt something like relief mixed with pity, and something else like fear. "Hey man," Aaron said, clasping his hand in a firm handshake. "How you holding up?"

"Fine," Becks said, a shadow passing across his face. But he quickly recovered and ushered them in, giving Eliza a quick squeeze when she reached out to hug him.

"No Whitney?" Eliza said. The house was immaculate: glistening baseboards (where Aaron's mom had always taught him to look first), scrubbed floors, clean countertops with nothing on them save a vase of flowers here and there. Whitney ran a tight ship, no doubt, but Aaron also knew that Becks had always pulled his weight and then some in that department—all the more since his retirement, when Aaron knew that his friend felt that he had to have some other way to prove his utility.

"Out running a few errands," Becks said. "She usually does in the morning—less busy at the stores."

"And you stay back and man the house," Aaron joked.

"She says it's easier if she runs them alone," Becks said. Eliza shot Aaron a warning look.

Becks offered them coffee, which both Aaron and Eliza agreed to, before they turned to pull open the window blinds to let in some natural light. "That's okay, isn't it?" Aaron asked. It was the one thing about the house that he couldn't stand—all the blinds closed, the place lit only by artificial overhead lights.

"Whit prefers to have them closed," Becks said, frowning. "We'll put it back before she comes?"

"Of course," Eliza said. "She probably just doesn't like anyone snooping."

"I'll keep an eye out," Aaron promised.

Aaron felt restless; as Becks made the coffee and Eliza made idle chitchat, he couldn't help but feel the weight of the awkwardness around them. But why? They were all old friends. Had Gina Tiller's death so changed them? Were their secrets really so poisonous, so insidious? Aaron sat down at the low coffee table next to one of the couches and rubbed his temples.

"You look like me," Becks said, grinning, as he handed Aaron a cup of coffee. "Headache?"

"No, man, just tired. You've been having headaches?"

Becks' face closed up. "Not recently," he said, taking the seat next to Becks as Eliza joined them. "No. Not really."

"I get headaches sometimes," Eliza volunteered. "Sometimes I'm just dehydrated."

Silence descended.

"So," Eliza said, trying to smile. "Becks, tell us how you've been since the party. Aaron and I were just talking about it— so tragic, with Gina."

Aaron winced.

"Tragic," Becks repeated. "Yeah." He paused. "I thought you didn't really like her, Lize."

"Oh! I-I mean, I didn't mind her," Eliza said. "She was— she was a nice girl, I guess. I hope you didn't tell the police that." And she laughed, a little too high-pitched, and Aaron looked sideways at her.

"I told that journalist that it wasn't your fault, what happened with—well, with the Tillers," Becks said. Aaron's head swung to Eliza, who blinked, freezing.

"I'm sorry?" she said, and before Becks could answer, "I'm not really sure what you mean, Becks. I don't have any problems with them."

Becks held her gaze while Aaron looked from one to the other. More secrets? Ones that he did not know? "Now if—" Aaron began, but Eliza cut him off.

"We really just wanted to check on you," she said quickly, easily. She even reached over and squeezed Aaron's knee, as if that would distract him long enough for her to change the subject (it did). "See how you're feeling, and see if there's anything we can do for you."

"No, I mean, I feel better, really," Becks said, sounding puzzled. "Ever since that night…I was sick after, really tired, but then since then…I don't know. It's like a weight has been lifted off of me."

"Because Gina died?" Eliza said sharply.

"No. No, I don't mean that—at least I don't think I do." He colored a little. "I wouldn't—I don't think I would —anyway."

"It's all good, Becks," Aaron said, a little too cheerfully. "Glad to hear you're feeling better—just think how good you'll feel once this whole thing is sorted, eh?"

The door to the house creaked open, and all three of them jumped up from the couch. Eliza recovered first, approaching the bewildered figure of Whitney with her arms outstretched, exclaiming how good it was to see her and how they were just talking about her. Becks and Aaron stayed together, back near the couch, both of them well aware of the strength of a crossed lover's wrath as they listened in.

"I told you that he wasn't ready for visitors," Whitney said coldly, entering the kitchen and depositing two large paper grocery bags onto the kitchen island. "He needs to rest."

"I know, Whit, but we know you, and you never ask for any help. We just thought we'd pop by—we didn't even know you wouldn't be here."

"You shouldn't have come," Whitney said. "You're going to tire him out."

"I'm fine," Becks volunteered, and looked chastened at a glance from Whitney.

Aaron moved to the kitchen, signaling to Eliza that they should go. "Real sorry, Whit," he said, as Becks' wife looked up at him. He could have sworn that her eyes swam with tears. "We didn't mean to bother you."

"It's fine," Whitney said. Her voice was husky. "Really. It's fine. We're—I'm—keeping it together."

Eliza reached out to comfort her, but Aaron shook his head. "If you need anything, you know where to find us," Aaron said.

Whitney nodded, turning her back to him as she began to unload the first bag into the fridge. Becks hurried over to help her.

Just as Eliza and Aaron reached the front door, Whitney called out to them. "Guys? I'm sorry. I—we really do appreciate it. Appreciate everything. It's just been a weird week, that's all."

"You don't have to apologize for anything," Eliza said. Aaron nodded and waved again, and then they were out in the cold air, in the bright sunlight, in the wide world free of that oppressive house.

Eliza shuddered. "Can you imagine? Being trapped in there?"

"Becks?"

"Whitney too. Worried about the press. Worried about what people are saying about her husband. It's enough to make someone go crazy."

They both exchanged a look, and Aaron shook his head. "Let's talk about something else."

Eliza drove them back towards his condo, fingers tapping nervously through the radio stations. Aaron felt chilled; it came to him, finally, that his friend really *was* in trouble. Something had happened that weekend, and Becks would not escape from it unscathed. Aaron could handle himself, but Becks...? The man had been through enough. It wasn't fair.

"What?" Aaron said, when he turned back to Eliza. "You look like you've seen a ghost."

Eliza didn't say anything. She continued to cycle through the stations, hazel eyes fixed on the road.

"They're not doing well," she said finally.

"No," Aaron agreed. "No, they're not. It's a serious situation. The police will probably talk to all of us soon." He paused. "I'm surprised they haven't already."

"Especially you, since you slept with her," Eliza said viciously. But she sighed and reached over to pat Aaron on the leg, dodging his attempt to squeeze her hand. "I'm sorry. I'm stressed. I don't mean to be throwing it back in your face like that."

Aaron said nothing, jaw tight.

"I'm also...feeling a little guilty," Eliza continued. Aaron turned to look at her, but she remained focused on the road. Was this why she was telling him this here? Because she didn't have to make eye contact? "I haven't told you everything."

Aaron's stomach somersaulted. If she told him about... then he'd have to tell her...and he wasn't sure he was ready...

"You know back when the press first started talking about how Becks maybe had CTE?" Eliza said, her voice catching. "Right after that tackle?"

"Yes."

"Well…Whitney just wouldn't listen to any of it. She said that it was an accident, that Becks didn't *mean* to do it. I told her to get Becks checked out, just in case, but she refused. For weeks. There was no talking sense into her."

"Eliza…"

"No, wait. I have to tell you this. So by then about six weeks had gone by, and the stories were dying off, and Whitney was still refusing to do anything but sit in that stupid house and try to call up their friends and figure out the 'next move' for Becks. Meanwhile, the only time I ever saw Becks, he was almost definitely depressed. Maybe more, I don't know. I keep telling her she has to address this thing, and she just ignores me. So I tried to help."

Aaron took in a long, slow breath.

"I called the press," Eliza said, voice breaking. "I just gave them a few anonymous quotes…stoked the fire a little bit, so that *someone* would have to check on him."

"Jeez, Lize," Aaron said. "Didn't you try the head coach first? Heck, you could have called me, or any of his teammates."

"You wouldn't have talked to him," Eliza said hotly. "He was still a liability to everyone at that point. No one wanted to speak to him. The coach would have had some junior associate come over and do a home check, and nothing would have happened. But when there was more media attention, Whit finally took him. They started seeing a doctor after that."

"After you made their lives more of a hell and forced their hand."

"I had to do *something!* I care about them."

"I do, too."

"But you would have let them rot in that house and done nothing," Eliza said. A tear spilled down the corner of her cheek. "Never mind. I don't mean that. Think whatever you want of me—I would do it again."

Aaron stared stonily out the front window. He thought to himself that this was far from the secret about the Tillers that he thought Becks was alluding to, back in the house. He thought that maybe that's what Becks had meant after all: that he knew Eliza had ratted on him to the press, and that he was getting her back. Was the sweet Becks capable of something like that? Maybe not the man Aaron had known, but this new version, this one hardened by exile and injury and shaped by bitterness...could he say for sure?

It's fine, Aaron thought to himself, crossing his arms as they drove back in silence. *Because Eliza isn't the only one who can keep a secret about the Tillers.* If Aaron was worried at all about the police questioning him, his one-night stand with Gina was the least of his concerns.

CHAPTER 26

*B*ecks was sleeping deeply.

His dreams were not unpleasant, for once: usually they involved some combination of being followed by something he could never see, going to football practice only to find the stadium empty and his head coach scowling at him with a look of hatred across his face, or (for reasons Becks didn't know) entering a deep, dark water and being pulled down, down, down.

But now his dreams were light and cheerful. He was playing football again—anything happy involved playing foot-ball—and he was eagerly anticipating the acceptance letter from a business school that, in real life, he would never get to attend. Somehow the Gina Tiller thing had been neatly cleared up in this dream: Becks remembered someone mentioning something about the case being solved, and that Gina Tiller was actually alive, and the whole thing had been a rather unfortunate misunderstanding.

Slowly, though, the dream began to shift. Becks felt rest-less, even in his sleep. He had sleepwalked a few times before —had since college—almost always accompanied by more vivid dreams. The world he was in grew sharper; Becks suddenly felt uneasy. "You're lying to me," he told his head coach, his voice dreamy and faraway. "Gina Tiller is dead. She died."

The coach made a face. "That's your problem," his head coach said. "No one believes you when you tell the truth, so no one is going to believe one of your lies."

"It's not a lie!" Becks protested. And then suddenly he was in another location entirely. Whitney was next to him, crying. "Whit?" Becks said, voice shaking.

"Becks!" Whitney cried. "Becks! Please, Becks! Go to bed. Just go back to bed."

"What?"

His mind stuttered; he was yanked out of the dream and blinked, feeling unsteady, like the world was slipping sideways from him. He blinked again and saw that Whitney was indeed in front of him, clutching her arms about her loose night-gown, tears streaming down her face. "Whitney," Becks said, taking a step towards her. Whitney flinched and took a step back. "Whitney, what's wrong?"

"Are you awake?" Whitney said tentatively. "Becks?"

"Yes. Was I sleepwalking?"

Whitney shuddered, the movement shaking her entire body. "Yes," she whispered. "Come back to bed."

They went together, padding away from the kitchen (how had he gotten to the kitchen?) and back to the bedroom. Becks noticed that Whitney climbed into bed as far away from him as possible, scooting to the edge of the mattress, surreptitiously sliding a pillow between them.

Becks' heart thumped in his chest. Maybe he was still dreaming. Why would his wife be afraid of him? He tried to say something, but Whitney, reaching out to squeeze his hand, said, "Go to bed, honey."

When he woke up in the morning, Whitney had already leapt out of bed to make breakfast and tea. She brought him a cup as he yawned and stretched, and perched on the corner of the bed. She was in a smart turtleneck and khakis today, and looked somehow younger, eyes too bright.

"Do you remember last night?" she said carefully, plucking at a loose thread on the comforter.

"I was sleepwalking, wasn't I?"

Whitney hesitated. "Yes."

"I'm sorry. Did I disturb anything? Break something?"

"No, honey."

Becks waited. The tea began to grow cold in his hands. "Then what?" he burst. "Just tell me, Whit."

Whitney took a deep breath. "You—you threatened me a bit, Becks."

"Threatened you?"

"Yes." Her voice was small and distant. "It wasn't—I mean, I knew you weren't—" Whitney swallowed. "It's not a big deal, hon. I just think, for now, maybe we sleep in different bedrooms. Until you've seen a doctor."

"I am seeing a doctor."

"Another doctor, then."

Becks felt a wave of cold rush through him. His immediate response was to deny: threaten Whitney? He would never. He had been having a pleasant dream, hadn't he? Nothing violent. Nothing that would suggest…

"Did I hurt you?" Becks said.

Whitney hesitated a fraction before saying quickly, "No. No, sweetheart, of course not."

"Show me your arms."

Whitney dutifully rolled up her sleeves, showing him the pale flesh. Becks grabbed her left forearm before she could draw down the sleeves and flipped it over, pushing the fabric up until he saw the soft trace of a fingerprint bruise on her skin, a deep blue. Whitney pulled her arm back.

"Your neck," Becks croaked.

"Honey, it's nothing."

"Whit. Please."

Whitney sighed and drew done one corner of her turtle-neck. Becks only saw the bruises for a flash, but it was enough. More dark fingerprints. Fresh bruises.

Whitney seemed embarrassed as she pulled her turtleneck back up. "You were sleepwalking," she said. "We're going to see a doctor and maybe get a new prescription. You'll just have to be more careful. Maybe…maybe take some melatonin or something, to help you sleep better."

He didn't know what to say. Again a part of him wanted to reject what she had told him. He wanted to shout at Whitney that it wasn't him, that why was she lying to him, why was she doing this to him? He felt rage bubble at the back of his skull. This couldn't be happening. Not now. And he had been feeling so good…

Becks collapsed back onto the bed. "Call Evan," he said.

Whitney watched him, still hesitating.

"Go," Becks said. "Call him. You shouldn't be dealing with this alone."

"Don't be dramatic, Becks."

"I'm not! Whit, please," he said, exhaling through his teeth. "I'm worried."

Whitney reached out and squeezed his hand. "I love you," she said. "We'll get through this." But her voice broke on the last word, and she moved out of the room and to the kitchen. Becks heard her dialing as he buried his face in his hands.

"Evan?" Whitney said. Her voice was tremulous. "Yes, I'm fine. Everything's fine. Listen, Becks and I are going to visit a new doctor soon. Yup, everything is all right…it's just…" She had the respect to at least not try to lower her voice, to act like she was talking behind Becks' back. "We had a little sleep-walking incident last night. So we're going to see a psycholo-gist, get on a new treatment." She paused. "Exactly. No, no need. I can handle it. Becks and I just wanted to update you." A pause again. "Are you sure? I think—well, that's fine, then. Thank you, Evan."

Whitney strode back into the room. "Evan's going to come visit," she said, with false cheer. "Won't that be nice?"

"Yes," Becks said dully. It was funny: the moment his football career had ended, Becks thought his life was over. Now he knew that the feeling was false, a mere shadow.

Now he knew what it *really* felt like.

CHAPTER 27

*R*ick waited until he saw Whitney's car pull out of the drive before he walked up and knocked on the door. For a few minutes, no one answered. Rick knocked again, louder this time. Just when he was about to give up, the door swung open, and a changed Becks appeared before him.

"Jeez," Rick said. "What happened?"

Becks looked dazed. He was still in pajamas, his hair tousled and his eyes heavy. "I don't have anything to say."

"What happened?" Rick repeated again. When he had last seen the ex-footballer, he had seemed fine—at least, not like this. Was the weight of the murder weighing on him? Had he finally decided to confess? A shudder ran through Rick. He reminded himself again that there was no reason to believe yet that Becks did it. That he didn't *want* to believe that Becks did it—no matter how much he fought against the impulse.

"Let me come in for a minute," Rick said. "You look terrible, man. I'll fix you a coffee."

"I can do that," Becks said, seeming confused as Rick pushed his way in. He felt a stab of guilt but reassured himself that he wouldn't abuse the footballer's head problems. He wasn't here to extract a quote; he was here to help, as much as a man like him could.

Rick followed Becks to the kitchen. The house was immaculate; Rick never felt at home in houses like this, which felt more to him like museums than actual homes. His eyes skirted over the weekly vitamin pill dispenser places neatly on the counter, over the glass jars of grains neatly stacked in one of the open shelves, over the television, still on, blaring some sports news program.

"Sucker for torture, huh?" Rick said.

"What?"

"Never mind. Where's the coffee? I'll make us a cup. You sit down."

Becks looked confused at this and rubbed his hair with one hand. "Sorry," he said, almost to himself. "I-I didn't sleep well last night. I'm going to—Whit is setting up another doctor's appointment."

"That's good," Rick said, a little too cheerily. "Get some sleeping pills if you need them, I guess?"

"I guess."

Becks ambled over to the couch; Rick set to work making coffee from the fancy, immaculately scrubbed machine in one corner. It involved feeding the blasted thing some sort of metallic pod in a star-shaped cutout and pulling a lever that made a disturbing gurgling and giggling sound. Finally, he managed to get a rather watery stream of coffee out of the machine and ended up splitting the batch between two cups, not trusting himself to wrestle with the contraption a second time. He brought the cups over to where Becks sat on the couch and turned the television off. Becks blinked at him.

"Seriously," Rick said, his stomach twisting. "Something happened, didn't it? You can tell me. Off the record, and all that. I'm not here to get a story."

He wasn't sure if Becks heard him, at least fully. The ex-footballer rubbed the back of his neck. "I always wanted a dog," Becks said. "Liven up the house, you know."

"Okay."

"Whitney doesn't want one. Says it's a lot of responsibility. I guess I can't really have that many, right now."

"I'm sure you're responsible enough to take care of a dog, Becks."

Becks smiled bitterly. "No," he said. And then, in a near whisper, "I hurt Whitney. When I was sleeping."

Rick felt another rush of cold go through him. "Hurt her how?"

"I...I don't know. Bruised her."

"Rolled over, or something?"

"No."

Becks didn't offer any more details, and Rick was too afraid to press. He was a fool, he knew he was, for wanting to think anything different than the obvious. He had seen the tackle: he had made himself watch it again on the way over, to prove to himself that the soft-spoken Daniel Becker was indeed capable of enormous, vicious violence when he wanted to be.

"Well, never mind that," Rick said. "I'm sure your wife is sorting it for you. In the meantime, I wanted to talk to you about your business partner. Evan Miller."

Becks perked up a little at the name. "About Evan?" He massaged his temple as he spoke.

"Yup. So you guys are starting your company here, right? In St. Clair."

"Yes."

"And you intend to keep it here."

"For now."

"For now?"

Becks shifted. It seemed like an effort for him to focus on the conversation. Rick guessed that his mind was still running over the events of the night before, struggling to piece them together. He felt a rush of pity, then chided himself for it. "For now, yeah," Becks said.

"Would it surprise you to hear that Evan plans to move the business to Florida?"

Rick expected the bomb to drop, for Becks to react, even in his sluggish state. But Becks did not look surprised at all.

Instead he asked, "Where did you hear that?"

"I heard it around. It's not a shock to you?"

"No. It's—we're not telling people about that, not yet."

Rick deflated. "So you knew."

Becks took a long breath, looking down at his cup of coffee. He blinked a few times. "Whitney doesn't want to stay in St. Clair, not long-term," he said. "She wants us to go to Florida. Evan, too. For the business. She has some family down there. We're not telling anyone yet because of the investors. I'm sorry," Becks finished, blinking. "Could you get me a glass of water?"

Rick walked to the kitchen to fulfill Becks' request, puzzled. He had been so sure of himself before. But the further he pried into Becks' life, the more mysteries and contradictions he seemed to find.

When he passed the water glass to Becks a minute later, he asked, "What about a clause in the contract, saying that Evan can move the company anytime he wants?"

Becks downed the water. Rick had to repeat the question two more times before Becks seemed to focus on it. "Oh," he said. "That. There's a clause about…anyway."

"You can tell me."

Becks gave Rick a skeptical look. He seemed exhausted, not thinking quite right. Lack of sleep, perhaps, and intense stress. "I shouldn't trust you," Becks said.

"You're smart not to trust anyone. But this is off-the-record, I swear. And I want to know for your own benefit. Anything like that in the contract?"

"I don't know who you've been talking to," Becks said

dubiously. "No. There's—there's something about decision-making if I'm—if one of us—" Becks sighed. "At first there was a clause that Evan would have the decision-making power in case of my...incompetence. But I had him change it. That either one of us would have decision-making power in case of another's...incompetence." He made a face at the word. Rick felt another stab of unease.

"Smart. You didn't want him calling you out specifically in the contract. Or trying to have you declared mentally unstable and taking it from you."

Becks shrugged. "Whitney agreed. She said it was better that way."

"Evan was okay with it?"

"Evan is okay with anything so long as the contract gets signed."

"Right, because you all signed it at the party, didn't you? Or right after?"

"No. Evan is coming by this afternoon to sign it. Some lawyers and witnesses are coming over, too."

Rick felt a fluttering in his chest. "Is that so," he murmured. "Well, is there any rush? Do you have to sign today?"

Becks gave him another dubious look.

"I'm just saying," Rick said. "There's no rush, what with the murder investigation and all."

"You think Evan will want to pull the plug if I'm arrested."

"No, I don't. I don't know him. I'm just thinking, what's the rush?"

Becks shrugged. "We've waited long enough," he muttered.

They sat in silence for some time. Rick tried to think; he still so badly wanted to find out the truth, and more than that, to find that the truth was not what he had feared. He had not been returning his editor's calls for the past few days;

he had sent over a half-hearted article about the "increasing questions" around the investigation, but it had barely mentioned Becks at all, instead focusing on the rest of the cast of characters who had attended the party. Rick had felt particularly hopeful that Sam was another prime candidate— Sam, who was an alcoholic, who had a history of assault, who disliked Gina. Or even Evan, who if he had not plotted to move the business to Florida behind Becks' back, at the least seemed a little too eager to get his hands on Becks' money. But what could Rick think when he had this version of Becks before him, the version that was confused, angry, defensive?

"Once the police find out what happened to Gina—" Rick began.

"She shouldn't have said anything about Whitney," Becks burst. "She shouldn't have insulted her. It wasn't right. It's not fair."

"No, she shouldn't have."

"Whitney and Evan are the only people who are still here for me," Becks said again, fiercely. He seemed to have forgotten that Rick was there. "They stood by me when no one else did. And she—she tried to tear them down. Why? Why did she care? Was she trying to get back at me?"

Becks' hands began to shake. Rick encouraged him to drink water and hurriedly went to refill his glass. Part of him felt like a coward for wanting to leave the house right then in case…no. Steeling himself, Rick brought the glass back to Becks and sat a little further down the couch from him.

"She shouldn't have done that," Rick said gently. "It wasn't any of her business. I'm sure she was just being herself…just messing around. It doesn't excuse it. But no one took those insults seriously. And you aren't the only one who disliked her."

Becks shook his head.

"Seriously," Rick continued. "The police will have their

hands full. You should have seen the way half the room looked at her."

"Like who?"

"Sam O'Nally, for one. You know he had an altercation with her before? And he has a history, too, and—" Rick stopped, realizing the same line of reasoning could be used to implicate Becks. Becks only shook his head.

"Sam's my friend," he said. "He—he didn't have to come out and support me. Not after everything that happened. But he did."

"Well one of your friends is a murderer," Rick said, and then wished he could take it back. Becks' hands shook again as he reached for his water glass. "I just mean—"

"It wasn't Sam," Becks said fiercely.

Silence descended again. Rick waited, heart rate picking up, wondering if the next words would come: *It was me.* Becks' breath grew rapid and shallow. He leaned back on the couch, pushing the heels of his hands into his eyes.

"You okay?" Rick said finally. Becks nodded without straightening. "Listen. If you need anything, you call me, okay? Where's your phone?"

Becks grunted and pointed to the table. Rick had him unlock it, feeling like some sort of co-conspirator. He didn't want to explain himself to Becks' wife and had a feeling that no one else in the Becker extended family would exactly understand his motives. He entered his number into Becks' contacts and handed it back. "You call me anytime you need something," he said.

"Why?"

"Because I don't think you did it," Rick said, not sure if he believed himself. But *because you're broken, just like me* didn't quite have the same ring to it. "You call me if you need anything, and maybe—I mean, I'm not telling you to keep secrets, but… I can't imagine Whitney would be thrilled."

Becks pocketed his phone and shrugged. "There's nothing

you can do anyway," he said, his voice almost mournful. "You should probably leave."

Rick did, suddenly feeling the need to get out of the oppressive house, away from the sad footballer and the potentially imminent return of his wife.

Death was in that house, Rick thought to himself as he left. Rick just didn't know whose.

CHAPTER 28

*E*van arrived at the Beckers' house at noon precisely, briefcase in hand. He knew that the lawyer and witnesses wouldn't be arriving until 12:30—knew, too, that the lawyer would certainly still be grumbling about having to make a home visit, because Whitney had insisted that Becks was not well enough to go out yet. He wanted time with both of them, alone, before the entire party arrived.

He knocked on the door, trying to take a deep breath. The whole last week had left him feeling rattled. Everything had been so promising…had been looking up so much….Why did Saturday night have to end so horribly? He knew he never should have invited that Gina Tiller woman. He realized it was unfair, but he felt almost like she had *schemed* to be murdered, that somehow, in some twisted way, it was at least a little bit her fault.

The door swung open, and Whitney stood on the threshold. She wore no makeup, and her hair was drawn back into a tight ponytail. She still looked beautiful, of course, beautiful and hard. Her eyes assessed Evan coolly.

"How is Becks?" Evan said, to cut the silence.

"I don't know if we should do this today," Whitney said. "He hasn't been well."

Evan felt his gut twist again. He didn't know what to say to Whitney. She knew just as much as he did how crucial it was that the business get moving. Otherwise, it would never get off the ground. And sure, they each had enough money to last them a few years—but after that? What about their future?

"Let me talk to him at least," Evan said. "As a friend."

"Evan—"

"Whitney, please. He shouldn't feel isolated."

She scowled at that, but after another few seconds of deliberation, moved aside to let him in. Evan hated the sudden change that had come over his friend's life because of that one stupid tackle. He was one of the only people who believed Becks, really believed him, when he said it had been unintentional. But the change in public opinion was too swift after that. Nothing could keep Becks' career alive. The rumors started almost as soon after, and Becks was left, in the snap of a finger, without a career, without a purpose, without any dignity. Even his sanity was questioned.

Evan knew it had been hard on his friend. He had tried to be there, over those first few weeks and months. It had been he who had suggested a business venture, thinking it might distract Becks. What it had grown into had been a surprise. By the time of the welcome party, Evan had his hands full, but he felt—he had to feel—that everything was in Becks' best interest, ultimately. It hadn't been easy, but then, nothing was.

He found Becks sitting on the couch, the lights dimmed low. His friend's arms were crossed as he watched some replay of a recent football game. Whitney came over and shut it off. "What did we agree about football?" she said.

"Don't mother him," Evan said.

Whitney gave him a harsh look. Evan ignored it and sat next to Becks. "Give us a minute, Whit?" Evan said.

But she punished him by sitting in the armchair adjacent

and folding her own arms, in an unconscious parody of her husband's position. Evan scowled and turned to Becks.

"How you holding up, man?" he asked.

"Fine."

"You don't seem fine. And I can tell you, I'm not. I'm pretty…shook, is that the right word? This whole thing has been a colossal mess."

That got Becks' attention. Becks looked up at him with dark-circled eyes. "For you, too, I guess."

"For all of us. It's a tragedy. Horrible. One of the worst possible things that could happen."

"I messed it up."

"*No.*" Evan's voice was emphatic. "Don't talk like that. Of course you didn't."

Becks shrugged.

"Listen. Nothing that happened at that party was your fault. Do you understand? Whitney here says you haven't talked to the police yet—when you do, don't give them any ideas."

"Don't worry; I don't remember much from that night."

Whitney and Evan exchanged a glance.

"It'll be okay," Evan said, squeezing Becks' shoulder. "Nothing to worry about, right? We've had a terrible setback—absolutely terrible. But we're going to work through it. We're going to move forward and put this all behind us."

"How?"

"Well, for one, we're going to sign those papers today. Finally become official, for the business. How about that?"

"No."

Evan's heart skipped a beat. "No?"

"No. I'm not signing any papers."

"Daniel," Whitney said, leaning forward. "Honey?"

"Let me handle it," Evan said brusquely. "What do you mean, Becks? Not feeling up to it today?"

"It's a stupid idea. Going into business with me. I'm poison."

"Don't say that, man."

"I am. Everything I touch gets destroyed. You don't want to start this with me. Really. I'm backing out."

Evan leaned back. "You've thought about this, then."

"Yes."

"And you're decided?"

"Yes."

Evan stood up and began pacing the room. "Becks," he said. "Look. I'll be honest. I want this—I *need* this—just as much as you. You're not doing me any favors, you understand? I put a lot into this. I want to do this with you."

"Don't put that on him," Whitney said, voice low and dangerous. "If he's not comfortable right now, he's not comfortable."

"You were doing fine without me," Becks said, with a weak smile. "And I think you'll be better off without me. I'll invest still, if you want. Give you some money to start your own company. But I don't want to be part of it."

"But that's basically what it is," Evan protested. "You're the funds, I'm the hands. I'll be working for you, Becks."

"No. I don't want to be a partner."

"So you'd rather just give me a bunch of money and be done with me?"

"Evan," Whitney hissed. "Give us a moment, please. And for God's sake, stop pressuring him."

Evan shook his head and rose. He couldn't begin to make sense of the stream of emotions running through him. The papers were almost signed—almost signed! Why was Whitney being a fool? Why was Becks on some new pilgrimage of martyrdom? It was nonsense, all nonsense!

He hadn't quit his steady, lucrative job on a whim. He had seen an opportunity, not just to make money but to help his friend. He had put his life on hold for Becks *and* for Whitney.

He understood, more than anyone, that Becks had a right to pull out whenever he wanted…but he had expected it early on, in the first few weeks and months when they had discussed the project. Not now. Not when there was so much more to lose. Not when it had blossomed into something greater than Evan had ever dreamed.

He walked to the kitchen and poured himself a glass of water. He tried to remember that Becks was all alone; his family had turned strange and scheming when Becks had made his money. His friends and fellow players had all left him after Becks was kicked from the league. Now Becks had only the last few shards of his dignity—for all the good they would do him, for however long they lasted.

What if Evan just called it off right now? What if he walked over to Whitney and Becks and announced that *he* was pulling out, that he was going to move to Florida without them and clean his hands of the whole mess? He thought with some satisfaction of the look of shock and even possibly hurt on Whitney's face—she had made things difficult for him recently—but then guilt took over, and Evan let the image dissipate. No, he couldn't do it because he couldn't bear the look of betrayal that would be on Becks' face. Not at leaving the company; Becks would probably welcome that. But at leaving *him*. And Evan knew that this look, this look of hurt, was something that he feared day in and day out. He would never let it happen. He would never let Becks think that one of the last people he trusted had hurt him, too.

Even if sometimes, Evan had no choice.

He downed the water and returned to Whitney and Becks. Whitney was still whispering in a low voice to her husband, who looked pale and a little disoriented. "Let's wait another few days," Whitney said, looking nervously at Evan. "How about that?"

"I'm not going to change my mind," Becks said.

"And you don't have to, honey. Friday morning, you can

make the call. Cancel for good, or we call in the lawyers again to sign. How's that, Evan?"

"Sounds like a plan," Evan said, with more enthusiasm than he felt. He didn't like the optics of it—forcing a sick man to sign papers. Maybe a delay *would* be best. But Evan didn't know. The stress of the last few days was getting to him; he could barely think straight sometimes.

Thank you, Whitney mouthed, and Evan just nodded. He reached over and squeezed Becks' shoulder, patted Whitney, and strode out the door. As he did, a weight seemed to lift from his chest.

That should tell me something, he thought. *But I'm just a glutton for punishment, aren't I?*

CHAPTER 29

*a*aron picked up the phone on the second ring. Next to him, Eliza looked up curiously.

"Becks?" she asked, seeing Aaron's stricken expression as he answered.

Aaron shook his head quickly. He struggled to listen. "Yes," he said, with a lump in his throat.

A few seconds later, Sam O'Nally came on the line.

"You have my number memorized, huh?" Aaron tried to joke, and then wished he hadn't.

"They let me use my phone," Sam said sullenly. His mouth sounded thick, stuffed with cotton. "Listen. I need someone to post bail."

"What happened?"

"Nothing!" Sam said. "Look, misunderstanding."

"What did they book you on?"

"Trespassing. Disorderly conduct. Like I said, nothing serious. But I need bail."

"What about your family, Sam?"

"You think if they were talking to me I'd call you?"

Aaron stood and began strolling towards another room,

hoping Eliza didn't see the movement as too suspicious. He felt her eyes following him as he went.

"Look," Sam said, frustrated, into the silence. "I don't want to be calling in this favor. But I've been a good friend to you. I could talk to the police, you know. Say things about your girl."

"You're threatening me."

"I'm not, man. Just saying that you should help me out. As a friend." He paused. "You do know, don't you? She's in on it. All but admitted it to me."

Aaron hung up the phone.

When he walked back to his kitchen, Eliza looked up from her magazine. "Who was that?" she asked. "Aaron?"

Aaron searched her face, trying to read any guilt in it, trying to understand. "Is there anything you're not telling me?" he asked.

Eliza folded her magazine and straightened. "Is there anything you're not telling *me*?"

Yes, Aaron thought. *But just to protect you.*

What in the world had they gotten themselves into?

CHAPTER 30

"He wanted money, that cockroach," Lyle Tiller said, face red as he half-lowered himself, half-fell into one of the high-backed library seats. He popped open the whiskey globe next to him and took out a glass, then snatched a decanter from the bookshelf behind him. Rick didn't bother to ask for a drink, nor did Lyle offer. "Drunk out of his mind. Stumbling around like some crazed ape. Said he knew things and he could help."

"Did he?" Rick said.

Lyle Tiller had called Rick the night before, in the early hours of Thursday morning, shouting into Rick's voicemail about a robbery and an arrest and *expletive expletive why can't you pick up the expletive phone.* He apparently had wanted an article to go out that morning, but had calmed down considerably by the time that Rick called him back at 6 a.m. Now, Lyle Tiller wanted blood.

"Did he help?" Lyle cried, almost spilling the whiskey as it sloshed in his shaking hand. "Of course he didn't!"

"I meant, did he know anything?"

"You think I wasted my time asking? I grabbed him by the scruff of his neck and dragged him out on the front lawn!"

Behind Lyle, one of the maids dusting the bookcases winced to hide a small smile. Rick sincerely doubted this version: Sam had a foot and a half at least on Lyle Tiller, and over a hundred pounds. Even drunk, Sam would be more than a match for him. More likely that Lyle had danced around as his security team had deposited the drunk Sam O'Nally outside. "Besides, he just wanted money," Lyle snarled, taking a long sip of his drink. The clock struck eleven a.m. "Kept ranting about how he knew about Eliza." Lyle scowled and glanced back at his maid. "That's clean enough! Leave us alone."

When the library was empty of all except the two of them, Rick asked, "He was referring to the allegations?"

Lyle's red color deepened. "You mean her lies? And when's the article on this coming out, anyway? What am I paying you for, to sit around?"

"You're not paying me," Rick reminded him.

"No? Oh—well, that's all right, then. But it's coming soon, I guess?"

"As soon as I can. But that's why Sam was here, to threaten you about Eliza? And ask for money to keep quiet, I'm guessing?"

"Probably. I didn't let him get that far." Lyle looked down into his drink. "He said—well. That perhaps Gina knew."

Rick pondered this. If Gina knew about Eliza's allegations about her father—what then? Would she have felt so defensive of him that she would have confronted Eliza? Would Eliza's friends—Aaron, or Whitney, or even Becks—have tried to warn Gina off to protect her? And Sam was what, a witness to it all? An eavesdropper? It didn't make sense.

"Do you think your daughter knew?" Rick said finally. "About—about the accusations?"

"I never told her that gossip," Lyle huffed. "She always loved her daddy."

Rick cringed.

144

"She thought the world of me," Lyle continued, swirling his whiskey around the tumbler. "She wouldn't have believed it, even if someone told her."

"You think maybe she argued with someone, when they said something to her."

Lyle's jaw tightened. "I-I don't know."

Rick nodded. He could tell that even the idea that his indiscretion had something to do with his daughter's death weighed on Lyle—but let it. Rick had little sympathy for a man who could not even admit that he had done wrong.

"Why don't you interview him, in jail," Lyle said tightly. "Figure out what he knows."

"You know all those conversations are recorded, don't you?"

"Why do you ask?"

"In case he says anything incriminating. Or incendiary."

Lyle frowned. "What are you implying?"

"Nothing. I was just letting you know. I was thinking of trying to meet with him again, anyway. I'm sure he could use a visitor."

"You'll send me the story, before you publish it?"

"Of course." If Rick wanted to. As long as he needed to stay in Lyle's good graces. Rick knew where his loyalties lay, and it certainly wasn't with this rich football team owner who thought he had a pet reporter in his back pocket.

He stood, while Lyle Tiller remained seated, eyes glazed as he stared out the window. It was something of a revelation when Rick thought, *I wouldn't trade places with you for the world.*

CHAPTER 31

$\mathcal{B}$ecks sank down into the cushions of his couch, stunned.

DNA evidence. That was what the cops had wanted to discuss. That was what the dark-eyed detective had talked to him about, when she had entered his house and spoken in a low, soothing voice to him about what they were investigating. Becks had done what Whitney had told him to do, whenever she was out of the house. "I can't speak to you without a lawyer," he had told the detective.

"That's okay," she had said. "I'll talk to you."

And she did. She told him about his DNA, and where it was found. After that, Becks didn't hear much of anything at all.

"Are you going to arrest me?" he blurted out when she finished speaking.

She gave him a look of almost pity. "We'll be in touch," she said. "I just wanted to let you know."

Becks couldn't quite believe it even now. He wondered, as he sat curled up on himself, if he had hallucinated the whole meeting. Certainly the world had felt cloudy that morning; certainly his head hurt more than it had in weeks, and he barely had an appetite. Even the detective had seemed to notice that he was unwell, and had looked at him with that awful sympathy that Becks had grown to despise. He wondered if he was truly going crazy.

Had he murdered Gina Tiller?

Sometimes, if he shut his eyes, he thought he could remember something. Of feeling so angry that night, so lost. And then—flashes, dream-like, so fleeting he wasn't sure if they were real or imagined—the image of a woman backing away from him, of his hands around her throat, of a scream, and then—

Becks dropped his face into his hands.

When Whitney found him, an hour later, he had somehow drifted off into an uncomfortable sleep. In his dreams he was locked up in jail, and Gina Tiller was next to him, her neck bruised and her eyes bright. "It's okay," she said cheerily. "You didn't mean to, right?"

"Becks!" Whitney shook him by the shoulders, and Becks gasped awake. His hands squeezed over Whitney's arms and she squealed, pulling away from him.

"Whitney," Becks said, horrified. He sat up quickly, and the room immediately began to spin. His wife looked frightened and took another step back.

"Are you okay?" Whitney said tentatively. "You were—you seemed upset. When you were sleeping."

"Fine." He rubbed at his eyes, trying to look alert, aware of how he was losing the struggle more and more as the days went on. He could feel Whitney pretending not to notice, pretending to dust something off of one of the armchairs, to give him a moment to recover.

"The police," Becks croaked. "They came, didn't they? When you were gone?"

"What?" Her voice was sharp, taut.

"They came. I'm sure they did." He pressed his fingers against his temples, scanning. "There," he said triumphantly, pointing to the glass of water that the detective had poured for herself. "She drank that. Stone—Detective Stone."

"I told you not to talk to them without an attorney, Becks," Whitney said. He could hear the barely contained panic in her voice. "I told you—"

"I didn't. She came in and spoke to me. I didn't say anything."

"What did she tell you?"

Again Becks pressed on his temples. It felt like his head was on fire. He needed some water, or an aspirin, or something. Whitney saw him struggle and rose, returning in a few seconds with a full glass.

"Drink," she encouraged him.

He downed half of it and sighed. "Something about— DNA evidence."

Whitney looked stricken.

For a moment the words hung between them: *DNA evidence*, solid and real and ugly.

Finally, Whitney said, "They can't prove anything. DNA can get on people at any time. We were all at the same party together, and—"

"My DNA, under her fingernails," Becks finished. "Under Gina Tiller's fingernails."

Whitney collapsed into the chair behind her, burying her face in her hands. Becks stood helpless as his wife shook with silent sobs, not lifting her face. *I'm sorry*, he wanted to say. *I messed up. I keep messing up. I'm sorry.*

CHAPTER 32

*E*liza went out for coffee while Aaron was at physical therapy. She felt like she was trapped in some awful nightmare and didn't know how to escape. Blackmail, murder, police investigations, career-ending injuries...all of it cascading down and so much of it landing on her shoulders. Why couldn't she just wipe her hands and be done with them all?

She saw the call from Whitney as she left the café with her smoked rosemary latte. "Whit," she said, climbing into her car. "I was just thinking about you guys."

The voice on the other end was muffled.

"Whit?" Eliza said, straightening as she turned on her car. "Whit, you there?"

She heard a distinct sniffle. And then, "Yes, I'm here."

"What's wrong?"

For a moment she heard nothing but more sniffling on the other end of the line. Then something garbled, including the words *DNA* and *police*.

"Whitney?" Eliza said, her own breath catching now. "Whitney? What's going on?"

A shuddering breath. "The police came by. Becks is saying

they told him—they told him that they found his DNA on Gina Tiller."

Eliza sat frozen, latte hovering in one hand. "But that could be anything. We were all at the party. We were hanging out, and—"

"His DNA was under her fingernails."

Eliza's mouth snapped shut. She squeezed her eyes closed. *Not good*, she thought. *Not good not good not good.*

Whitney was now crying on the other line. She started blubbering again, nonsense that Eliza couldn't quite make out. Something about *failing him* and *not protecting him* and *not able to do this much longer.*

"I'll come over later," Eliza promised. "We'll go out for drinks. Let Becks rest. It will be fine. You have a good lawyer for him?"

"Yes."

"Good. You called her? Or him?"

"Yes. We're chatting tomorrow."

"Great. We'll get a handle on this. Don't worry."

"Eliza, I—I just…. If something were to come out…"

"One thing at a time," Eliza said firmly. "We'll worry about that when it happens."

"It's just all ruined," Whitney said. "It wasn't supposed to end up like this, you know? When I met Becks…even when that tackle happened…I thought we were going to be okay. I really did." Whitney began crying again. "It's my fault," she said. "I didn't protect him."

"That's absolute nonsense and you know it." Eliza swallowed, not sure what else she could say. She felt her own share of guilt for everything: for letting time and distance slowly pull them apart, for not checking on Whitney more, for not going over there, every week, every day, after Becks' fall from grace when Whitney needed her the most. Oh, she had checked on her, of course, sent flowers, sent texts, but maybe if she had done more…maybe if Eliza had stepped up…maybe none of this would have happened.

"What's that?" Eliza said, as Whitney mumbled something else into the phone.

"Nothing," Whitney said, sniffling. "I have to go. I'll see you tonight."

Eliza tried to ignore the foreboding feeling in her chest as she hung up.

CHAPTER 33

*T*he fact of the matter was, everyone had it wrong.

Rick paced the length of his apartment, mind whizzing. He wondered how everyone could have overlooked it—why everyone was so quick to jump to Daniel Becker as the culprit. Maybe because people were always obsessed with the mighty falling, with the narrative of the golden child corrupted and ruined.

Rick knew about the DNA evidence, of course. That was the first thing Becks had told him when Rick had called. "It doesn't matter," Rick said, a little thrown off but still high on his own breakthrough. "It can be explained away. You don't remember doing anything like that, do you?"

"I don't think so…"

"I'm calling in some favors," Rick assured him. "We'll figure this out. Don't lose hope, okay?"

Becks had made a noncommittal noise in response, and Rick had hung up, still feeling optimistic. But his optimism was tinged with restlessness and almost desperation…the clock was ticking, and he only had so long to prove Daniel Becker innocent.

The whole case had reinvigorated Rick. He felt a way he

hadn't for years, not since before he had abandoned his dreams in order to make a living. He felt...*good*. Ethical. Not riding a story until the bitter end, squeezing drop after drop from it, pandering to all of the gossip sites and the editors that he hated and the people he had to work with to get one measly little check in one to six months. He was searching out the truth and being careful about it.

Now, he was ready to share it.

Rick checked his watch and made for the door. There was just one final detail he wanted to check, and he had called in every favor he had ever had to get his hands on it. Rick wrapped a scratchy scarf around his neck and tugged on a coat before heading outside, warming his hands with his breath.

He was almost to his car when he saw her. Rick jumped, and then, wildly, felt a stab of fear. This he quickly got over (it was replaced instead by sheepishness), and Rick said, "Mrs. Becker. How can I help you?"

Whitney was parked behind him, a black ski coat hugged tight over her chest, her hair pulled into a bun with one wisp falling loose, sticking to her glossy lips. For a moment she said nothing; then she tucked the wisp of hair behind her ear and shook her head.

"I know you've been talking to my husband," she said. "I want you to stop."

Rick kept that stupid friendly grin that he had greeted her with on his face. He didn't quite know what to say next— denying it would be stupid, but admitting it would be stupider. "I certainly don't want to upset you," he said finally.

"Then stop talking to him. He has enough on his plate without some—without some *story* coming out."

"That's not at all what I'm interested in, ma'am. I'm trying to help, actually, by—"

But she laughed harshly on the word "help." "You think you're the first person that told me that you're trying to 'help' my husband?" she said. "I don't want anyone's help. I know that I'm looking out for his best interests. And I've learned that I can't trust that anyone else feels the same."

Rick wanted so badly to tell her. He wanted to lay the theory that he had before Becks' wife and see her eyes gleam first with suspicion, then with doubt, and finally with hope. He wanted her to share in his excitement. But he had to be patient. He couldn't risk anything going wrong, not at this stage.

So instead he said, "Understood. I'm sorry."

She didn't seem to buy the fake apology, her eyes staying narrowed at him. "I blocked you on his phone," she said. "If you try emailing him, I'll do the same thing there, too. And if you show up at our house, I'll call the cops."

"Seems excessive."

"I have to protect him," Whitney said fiercely. "I'll do whatever I have to."

Rick nodded. Without another word Whitney climbed into her car and drove off. Rick watched her go, feeling a churning sense of unease. It was more than obvious that Whitney Becker thought her husband had gone mad. And personally, Rick agreed with her. But did Whitney Becker also believe her husband was a killer?

And what lengths was she willing to go to in order to protect him?

CHAPTER 34

*A*aron walked out of physical therapy with his bag slung over his shoulder, feeling lighter than he had in days. He had finally, today, felt the first glimmer of hope that he'd be able to play in this week's scrimmages without completely embarrassing himself and tipping off his teammates that something was amiss. It hadn't hurt, of course, that he had been able to skip the first few practices this week due to the investigation, making excuses about police interviews and statements and the like, allowing himself time to heal outside of his coach's hawk-like eyes.

But he knew that there was something else he needed to do. Something he had been putting off for a long time.

"You look cheerful," Eliza said, handing him an iced coffee. "Go well?"

"Very well."

"So you'll make it through, you think."

"The next week? Yeah. I think so. All thanks to you."

Eliza shrugged off the compliment as she always did and started to drive back towards Aaron's apartment. He had always appreciated that about her, her cool efficiency, her no-nonsense style. They hadn't worked out as romantic partners, but he'd be a fool if he didn't see that Eliza was a great team-mate. This week alone, she had driven him to almost all of his appointments, set up his training, negotiated the rates, fielded off police and press inquiries, all the while working her own job and dealing with her own stress. Aaron would offer to pay her again, at the end of the week, if not in cash (as she already had refused), then in tickets, or something else she wanted that he could give her. And he would repay her for her friendship tenfold in the future.

He just needed to get something off of his chest first.

"Whitney is having a hard time," Eliza muttered. "She called me today."

"Yeah?"

"Yeah. She feels like she's letting Becks down. Seems like she thinks—well. That it's not going to go well for him."

They sat in silence for a few moments, letting this sink in. Aaron shifted uncomfortably.

"We'll just have to see," he said finally. "We'll hope for the best."

Eliza sighed.

"I also want to talk to you," he said, clearing his throat. "I've been meaning to for a while."

Eliza sent him a sideways glance as she drove. "That doesn't sound good."

"It's nothing that you don't know already. Well—not the first bit, anyway. Obviously my wrist is going to get better, soon."

"Yeah, if you ever let it heal properly."

Aaron half-grinned. "Well, I'm working on it. To get these sponsorships. Thanks again for helping me out with that. You're the only person—well, Lize, you're frankly the only person I'd trust to do all of that. To not panic or tell anyone. The only person I'd trust to actually help me, no strings attached."

"I *bet* you wish there were strings."

Aaron snorted, not sure if he got the joke and not wanting to press it. He liked Eliza when she was friendly—he wanted to keep it that way. "Yeah, maybe. But look. There's another part that I haven't really told you."

He watched Eliza's expression out of the corner of his eye. Her fingers tapped against the steering wheel, and her face, though it still held the ghost of a passing smile, looked almost frozen. She was nervous, Aaron realized. About what?

"My wrist will be fine eventually," he said carefully. "I just —some other stuff won't be."

"Other stuff?"

"I got some old injuries, Lize. You remember a bit—my knee? My right shoulder?"

"I thought those were fixed."

He ran his tongue behind the back of his teeth. "Yeah— sort of. Nothing ever gets fixed when you're playing pro football. Not really."

Eliza snuck another sideways glance at him. "So you're telling me that you're going to retire soon. After you nab the sponsorships?"

"*If* I do—then yeah. Maybe."

She nodded slowly, taking it in. Aaron tried not to fidget as he waited for her response. He hadn't realized until he had spoken the words just how important her opinion was to him, just how much he wanted her approval, or at least, her acceptance.

"That sounds like it'll be for the best," Eliza said finally. "Have you thought exit strategies? What are you going to do after? What do your finances look like?"

Relief washed over him. "I'm working on it. I thought maybe—well, I wanted to brainstorm with you a bit. Get your advice."

"As long as you're not about to ask me for a loan." She softened the sentence with a grin as she shot a glance at him. "Then yeah. Of course, Aaron. I'm here for you."

I'm here for you, too, Aaron thought. *Though maybe in some ways that you never wanted me to be.* He felt a shot of foreboding. No, he wouldn't think of it right now. He would get through this first. Then he would tell her.

They spoke a little bit about savings accounts and investments, about day jobs and transitions. Eliza had a few suggestions for him, some of which he liked and some of which he absolutely loathed. She offered to make introductions; they agreed to set up a few times in the next couple of weeks to meet up. It felt to Aaron like they were finally hitting their stride—they had been terrible in a relationship together, had brought out the absolute worst in each other. Eliza had become neurotic and compulsive to make up for Aaron's laziness and procrastination. He had criticized her for being overbearing and unadventurous; she had criticized him for being childish and without foresight.

Now, though, they had somehow arrived back at the place they had first been when they had met each other: Eliza smart, organized, and clever, and Aaron agreeable, open, and curious. It could stay this way, Aaron thought. If they didn't try to mess it up again by dating. If they just let each other be what they needed in each other's lives—nothing more, nothing less.

Even if Eliza *still* was the best-looking woman he'd ever seen.

"And Greg, you remember him from the party, don't you? He always hires athletes for his firm. You should follow up with him. You did meet him, didn't you?"

"I'm sure I did. I talked to everyone at the party, practically. Except Gina."

The mention of her name shattered the mood. Eliza stiffened, and Aaron cleared his throat self-consciously. "Sorry," he said. "I just mean—well, I avoided Gina. Gina is... was...difficult."

"Let's not talk about her, please."

"No, of course not. I just meant that, well, the whole *family* can be a lot to deal with, sometimes." Aaron felt himself treading on dangerous water. "That's all. And I did my best not to talk to her, really. As little as I could, anyway. She's not…she's just——"

"Let's not speak ill of the dead." Eliza's knuckles were now white as she gripped the steering wheel. "That's all behind us, okay?"

"Yes, but——" Aaron struggled. He didn't want to speak poorly of Gina. He didn't want to say what he really felt, that if he had to pick one person at the party to be offed that night, it would be her. Eliza might take that the wrong way. She might think that he thought…well. It was terrible of him, more terrible because of his past transgression. But Gina Tiller was a selfish and cruel person. He was sorry that she had been killed, but there was one part about her murder that he would never be sorry about.

Aaron swallowed. It was time.

"Look, Lize," Aaron said, as she took the steep highway exit towards his condo. He knew she wouldn't come up to chat if he asked her, knew that she just wanted the conversation done as soon as possible. He had to get this out now. "There's one more thing that I have to tell you."

"Oh, God," Eliza whispered.

CHAPTER 35

$\mathcal{R}$ick arrived at the police station and parked in the back, as instructed. When he had first moved to St. Clair, he couldn't believe how close the place was to the high school, and at first thought it cute and almost quaint, as if the worst offenses in the town were kids smoking something questionable in the stadium bleachers.

Years in St. Clair had taught him otherwise.

But Rick was an infrequent visitor to the police station, and he wanted to keep it that way. The man who had agreed to help him owed a big favor to Rick's sister's best friend, who apparently had so little use for it that she had bequeathed it to Rick (after a copious amount of begging).

He walked inside and told the receptionist who he was there to see, then went and sat on one of the low wooden benches near the door. He could barely keep his legs from shaking, up and down, up and down. This one confirmation of Rick's theory would be enough to run the story. From there, the police could deal with it as they may—certainly the cop showing Rick the evidence would take it to someone who could make use of it. Who could arrest Sam O'Nally and start the long process of securing justice for Gina Tiller.

And Becks would be free.

It didn't matter if Whitney Becker blocked all of Becks' devices so that Rick could no longer contact him. Rick would still do his duty for the ailing football player, and Becks would be able to tend to his health with a clear conscience. Whatever friendship they had struck up would have served its purpose, and both Becks and Rick could move on to new ventures with their heads held high.

Minutes passed. Rick began to worry that he had gotten the time wrong; he checked and double-checked his texts. He wondered if perhaps the cop wasn't in today, or if some emergency had happened pulling him away from his desk. He debated whether he should get up and ask the receptionist to check on the cop, before resolving to wait another ten minutes. As a rule, Rick tried never to piss off the receptionist.

The door opened. From the hallway walked a tall, ginger-haired cop with bright blue eyes, a crooked nose, and slumped shoulders. "Fales?"

"Rick," Rick said, rising and extending one hand. The cop shook it warily. "Thanks again."

The cop said nothing, only turned and walked back down the hallway. Assuming he was to follow, Rick hurried to stay on his heels. They moved to a small, windowless room with a beige carpet, a low wooden table, and two folding metal chairs. "Wait here," the cop instructed Rick. "I'm going to get my laptop."

Rick sat. There were also no mirrors in the room, so he didn't have to worry about the whole two-way mirror scenario, but still his eyes wandered, looking for any little opening through which a camera might point. He thought about what it would be like to be interrogated. He thought about whether, in a few days or a week or more, he *would* be, in a space exactly like this, as cops pumped him for more information about what he had seen the night of Gina's death. Except then, after today, he would feel confident about

166

telling them everything he knew. He would have no problems explaining about Becks' nap, about Becks' disoriented state, just minutes before Gina Tiller was found. Because by then, the cops would have arrested the right guy.

The cop returned. Rick's sister's friend had referred to him as "Billy," but Rick wouldn't dare try to veer from "William." Come to think of it, he wouldn't even go for first names—Officer Heitman would be the safest bet.

"Okay," Officer Heitman said, sliding into the seat opposite Rick. He tilted his computer so that both of them could see the screen. "I've got it all on here. You just have to tell me what exactly you're looking for."

"Exterior shots of the house," Rick said. "Around the pool."

"They're all exterior shots. Security cameras, you know?"

"Right—well. The pool. The back of the house."

The cop nodded and began to sort through the files. Rick wondered how much trouble the cop would get in if someone saw what he was doing. He wondered why the man had risked it at work, why he couldn't have taken the laptop down the street and shared it with Rick at Wolf Claw Coffee, for that matter. Or would the punishment have been worse for taking evidence off of police property? He didn't want to know and didn't want to press.

Instead he watched as Officer Heitman sorted through clips of the many security cameras on the outside of the Eastwick mansion. They saw dozens of partygoers, strolling outside for a smoke, mostly, or else hurrying with their arms wrapped around their bodies as they moved from one door to another, crossing the wings of the mansion via the back courtyard. Rick recognized some of the faces, but most were unfamiliar. He waited as the tapes rolled on, at a fast-forwarded rate, moving inexorably to the time stamp that would clear Becks.

Rick had thought of it the night before. Where had Becks

gone in the mansion, in those moments before he had come to rest on the staircase, sleeping? Upstairs killing Gina might be the obvious answer—but it was the wrong one. Becks had looked worn, and tired, and exhausted, all signs of someone who had been out in the cold too long. Rick hadn't touched the football player, but he was sure that if he had, he would have felt the remnants of the chill on Becks.

Naturally, if Becks had wandered outside, where would he be found? In the backyard, on the surveillance tapes, almost *exactly at the time of the murder.*

And—though Rick wasn't greedy, and certainly wouldn't depend on it—he wouldn't mind a little extra footage of Sam O'Nally after the murder. Maybe walking to the pool while pulling out his hair. Maybe leaning far enough over the balcony that the camera caught an image of his hand, and his cufflinks, and something identifiable.

"How much left?" Rick said anxiously.

"Halfway through," grunted Officer Heitman.

They watched as the night deepened with impossible speed, moonlight streaming over the pool. Rick felt his chest tighten. *Come on come on come on,* he chanted to himself, digging his nails into the palms of his hands. *One glimpse. One glimpse, at the right time—*

"Stop!" Rick said, but Officer Heitman had already spotted the figure and was rewinding. Rick's heart almost burst out of his chest. A tall man in a suit was just walking into the frame. "It's him," Rick cried. "It's him."

Officer Heitman leaned in closer, squinting. "It's someone," he said. "But that's not Daniel Becker."

CHAPTER 36

*W*hitney was keeping something from him.

That was all that Evan could conclude, after days and days of thinking about it. Of pondering why now, all of a sudden, Whitney was so eager to postpone the contract. She was trying to figure some way to get them out of it, perhaps. She had gotten cold feet. Or worse...

He would talk to her, soon. When he got the chance—whenever this whole Gina Tiller situation blew over. The frustrating part was that they seemed no closer to this end: Evan had received his first visit from a detective that very morning (and had been surprised it took them that long), and would not be shocked if they followed up a half-dozen more times.

He had to assume this: Whitney was afraid, because she thought that the police were circling around Becks. Why she should be afraid Evan didn't know; even if the police *did* move in that direction, surely they'd realize over time how wrong they were. Becks would be cleared, if not in two days then in two weeks. And then? Would Whitney see what her delays had cost them?

These thoughts swirled in Evan's head as he drove away from the police station and parked outside of Wolf Claw, where he said he would meet Sam O'Nally. Posting bail had not been his favorite experience—part of him wasn't even sure if he would get that money back; he supposed it depended on Sam's desperation.

But Sam also sounded like he knew something. And right now, Evan could use a little intelligence.

Heck, Evan thought to himself grimly, *maybe he was having a drink with Becks out back and wants us to pay for the alibi.*

It was a rosy-colored hope, but Evan clung to it as he waited. How wonderful it would be if in one fell stroke, the world could be righted! His hopes could be restored, his plans reinvigorated.

If only he could figure out what Whitney was keeping from him…

A knock on the car window sent Evan jumping. He smiled sheepishly and unlocked the door, and Sam O'Nally climbed in.

The man stank; he wore a stained white t-shirt and dark jeans, and his hair was a greasy mess, tied into a knot at the back of his head. He was entirely too large for Evan's car; his head had to tilt forward so as not to hit the roof, and his legs came nearly up to his chest. Evan heard the familiar buzz of the seat adjuster: after putting the seat all the way back and reclining it as far as it could go, Sam O'Nally at least looked like he could sit for fifteen minutes without cramping—but probably no more.

Good, Evan thought. *I don't want him to get too comfortable.*

"So you grabbing coffee for us or what?" Sam said.

"I thought you'd prefer to stay out of the limelight."

"Could use a coffee."

"Raincheck."

Sam grunted. But he seemed to remember that Evan was responsible for his bail and his freedom, or at least, he decided not to push his luck. "Fine. You driving us somewhere?"

"Your place. What's the address?"

Sam sighed loudly and gave it to him. "At least a drive-thru, man," Sam said. "I'm starving."

Evan agreed to go to the local burger drive-thru that was city-side, assuming that he would be paying for Sam and himself. They rode there in silence: Evan then ordered a small fries and Sam ordered two cheeseburgers, a large fries, an extra large soft drink, and five orders of chicken nuggets. "And do you have any pies?" Sam said, leaning over Evan to be heard on the drive-thru speaker.

"Apple, cherry, or chocolate."

"Two apple and one chocolate."

"That's all then?"

Sam pointed at Evan, who said, annoyed, "That's all."

Sam grinned.

"So you're still eating like an athlete, I see," Evan said, when they had driven away. He had considered asking Sam to wait to eat until they got to his place, then decided the battle wasn't worth it. Still, he winced as Sam slurped noisily at the burgers and dropped a half-dozen fries on his first grab for them. "Still work out a lot?"

"This is half of what I used to get," Sam said sullenly. "Hold on. I can't talk and eat at the same time."

They arrived fifteen minutes later outside Sam's door. Evan was always surprised to see that all ex-footballers didn't live like Becks did, though he knew he shouldn't be. Sam's apartment was part of a grungy, concrete complex with dirtied windows and crumbling roofs. Only the smallest green spider plant hanging outside the front door gave the place any sort of warmth. Evan complimented him on it as they parked, and Sam grunted, "Not mine."

"So," Evan said as Sam balled up his trash. "Before you go in. I had a couple of questions for you."

"Figured," Sam said, grinning. He still had ketchup smeared over one lip.

"You told me when you called that you had something important to say to me."

"I said I knew some things you probably were curious about. That you'd have a *vested interest* in, if you know what I mean."

"Yes, I remember you using that phrase." *With as much pride as if you'd learned it yesterday*, Evan thought with annoyance. "So? What is it?"

"You really want to know?"

"I think me posting your bail and driving you home pretty much shows you what I think."

Sam looked out the front windshield, seeming to consider. He had a mischievous look in his eye—no, not mischievous, *scheming*. Evan suppressed a shudder.

"Come inside, then," Sam said.

"What?"

"Come inside with me. I'll tell you there. Not out here."

"Why?"

Sam made a frustrated noise. "Because it's not the kind of thing you want anyone to overhear, you understand me?"

Evan frowned. "There's no one around. No one would overhear us in a car."

"I got nosy neighbors. Besides, it's easier if I show you something."

Evan again felt that prickle of foreboding. *No thanks*, he wanted to say. *I prefer not to enter the apartments of alcoholic ex-footballers with a criminal record.* But he was here now. And he wanted to know. He needed to know, so, so badly.

"Fine," Evan said, trying to sound braver than he felt. "But I can't stay long."

"Oh," Sam said with a wolfish grin. "It won't take long. Trust me, it won't."

CHAPTER 37

"What do you mean, it's not Becks?" Rick said sharply, leaning closer. He had already been thinking of all the people he would tell the good news to after revealing it to Becks—Lyle Tiller, for one, and then his editor. Rick would collect the payout, and the paper would run a story that would finally clear Becks' name.

But how could the figure on the tape *not* be Becks?

Officer Heitman sniffed and leaned away. He tapped the frozen screen, where a hulking man was walking out to the pool deck. "Watch here." He went frame by frame; the man never turned around, but he did tilt his head up and to the left as he walked. Or stumbled, really—in slow motion, Rick could see more clearly the awkward movements of the man.

The profile was not Becks at all. The nose, the chin, the hair were all wrong. Rick felt himself deflate.

"You know who it is?" Officer Heitman said. He was sitting up much straighter now, alert and almost frightened.

"Do *you*?"

"Of course not," Officer Heitman snapped. "I'm not working the case."

Rick sucked in a breath. "Sam O'Nally," Rick said. "Keep playing it."

Officer Heitman turned back to the screen, hesitating. Rick could feel him trying to decide whether to run to get another detective or to keep going. "Just the next few seconds," Rick said. "Then I'll get out of your hair, and you can go hand this off to the right person."

"I'd better not," Officer Heitman said peevishly. "Not if I want to keep my job instead of explaining why I've taken an evidence tape."

Rick shrugged sheepishly and indicated for Officer Heitman to continue. Again the officer looked conflicted, but after another few seconds of hesitation, hit the "play" button.

This time, Sam O'Nally moved in normal speed. He turned, his mouth slightly parting as he looked up towards what could only be the balcony. Rick thought he looked surprised—though the angle made it impossible to tell. He seemed to mouth something—Officer Heitman paused and played it back a few times.

"What the," Rick said.

"What?"

"*What the.* That's what he's saying. He's looking up and saying *What the*, like *What the heck.*"

Officer Heitman played it one more time, confirming the theory. The video continued on.

Sam O'Nally sprang back. The angle of the camera didn't capture Gina Tiller's fall, but it was obvious that this was what Sam was reacting to. He nearly jumped out of his skin; his hands went up to his hair, and he shook his head once, twice, as if denying the reality of what had just happened.

Then he ran.

"Holy…" Rick said. His mind was spinning. Sam O'Nally had seen the murder. Sam O'Nally had *witnessed* Gina Tiller being tossed off that balcony.

Which meant Sam O'Nally was not the killer.

And the killer could be anyone...or one person in particular.

Rick felt his whole theory unraveling before him. It couldn't be. Something had to be wrong. His mind fought to keep hold of his original ideas. Perhaps Sam was reacting to something else...perhaps the security footage was of a different night...perhaps this was a doctored video from a crooked cop trying to extort him for...for...

The video cut to black.

"That's it?" Rick cried. "That can't be it. Didn't Eliza Vorne find the body?"

Officer Heitman clicked on the video and typed a command on his keyboard. The video skipped back thirty seconds; they watched as the still frame continued on, then suddenly stopped, cut off.

"Did the film run out?" Rick cried.

"It's all digital. Of course not."

"Then what?"

Officer Heitman clicked a few more times, and they rewatched the end of the video. "Someone must have cut it," he muttered. "Cut the feed. Disconnected the camera."

"Why?"

Officer Heitman gave Rick a scathing look. "I can think of a few reasons."

"Is there another angle? Another camera to show what happened?"

"I'm checking."

They sat in silence for a few more minutes as Officer Heitman clicked around, looking for something, anything, that would give them answers. Rick felt his chest constrict; he had been so close, and now? Now he didn't know what to believe.

"There's nothing," Officer Heitman said finally. "That's the only camera. O'Nally must have seen something, and..." The police officer chewed the inside of his cheek.

"Have the detectives on the case seen this footage?"

Officer Heitman seemed distracted, so Rick repeated his question. "Hmm? No. We received the tapes this afternoon. Some trouble over contacting the owner, I think, since the house changed hands recently. Sorry, you have to go," Officer Heitman said, seeming to come to a sudden decision. "I have to show this to them. Now."

Rick rose. He felt a little dizzy. *There could be another explanation*, his mind tried to whisper to him, but what? Sam O'Nally was not the murderer. Becks' DNA was found under the woman's fingernails. Rick needed to stop hoping for a better end to the story. He needed to start facing the truth.

CHAPTER 38

*E*van left Sam's apartment, his whole body shaking. He could feel Sam watching him from the window, no doubt still staring at him with that wolfish grin.

He felt sick. He didn't want to think—couldn't think, not right now. He had to leave, first of all, and then he had to find Whitney. He had to find Whitney and talk to her. To protect her.

Why why why, Evan chanted to himself as he buckled himself into his car. It wasn't fair. It was all just—

A mess.

Part of him thought that he should call Aaron first. Tell him what Sam had been threatening. He was never friendly with Sam, but Aaron and Becks were. But Evan had no idea how Aaron would react, and so he nixed the plan.

But there was hope. If Evan could talk to Whitney. If Evan could find her. Whitney would know what to do. And Becks? Evan squeezed his eyes shut and turned the car on.

And maybe people wouldn't believe an alcoholic anyway. Maybe Sam O'Nally wasn't the reliable witness he pretended to be.

If only Evan could talk to Whitney...

CHAPTER 39

"There's one more thing I have to tell you," Aaron repeated, as Eliza pulled into the security gate of his condo complex. Aaron reached over to wave to the security guard, who motioned them through.

"I don't know if I want to hear it," Eliza said, jaw tightening. "Seriously, Aaron. I don't know if—"

"Please, Eliza?"

She parked and then looked at him, her face pale, almost supplicating. "Haven't I helped you enough?"

The question confused Aaron, who frowned. "Of course, I just—Eliza, you should know this. Really."

Eliza seemed to struggle within herself. Finally, she sighed, a long, whistling sound, and motioned for him to lead the way in.

Aaron's throat grew dry as he led Eliza across the parking lot, up the elevator, and down the hall to his condo. Part of him thought about reconsidering—about leading Eliza into his place, grinning at her, and making it seem like he had only tried to get her to come up for some other reason. But he was too nervous now to pull off the joke, and besides, this was what he had steeled his nerves for. Eliza had been there for him, this past week, and it was time that he came clean.

About everything.

They settled down to business almost immediately. Eliza took a seat at his counter, and Aaron stood across from her, leaning his elbows on the quartz countertop and biting his lower lip.

"I'm ready," Eliza said quietly.

"It's about Lyle Tiller."

Eliza blinked, her eyes fluttering. He could see her wrists stiffen as she struggled not to react.

"I know that he came on to you, in that interview," Aaron said. Even saying the words made him angry all over again— the idea that that fat old slob of a man thought, because he had a large bank account and a team of lawyers, that he could put his hands on a woman in his power made Aaron want to rip the man apart. He had come close. "I know that he was…inappropriate."

"How?"

Aaron shrugged. "I just heard, eventually."

"Whitney must have told you. Or told Becks, who told you."

"It doesn't matter," Aaron said, though this was uncomfortably close to the truth. "But I found out. And I—I went over there. To talk to him."

He saw the fear in Eliza's face, the very reason why he had not told her for so long. He was not ashamed of what he had done, would not take it back for the world, but he knew that Eliza would never want him to know. That it would embarrass her, the way it embarrassed every person who had ever had their dignity assaulted. That she would prefer to bury it and never talk about it again—least of all with an ex-boyfriend.

"So I go to his office and ask to see him. I didn't think he would let me in, if I'm being honest. I certainly wouldn't have. But he does, almost immediately, and I come in and he's just surveying the city skyline as if he didn't have a care in the world. Asks me if I'm having any problems with the coach or the team, as if anyone ever comes to him about that nonsense. I say no. He asks if I came to share good news. I say no. He asks if I came to share bad news. I said no, not exactly, but I don't think you're going to like what I have to say."

Eliza looked a little sick, now. Her gaze was lowered, and she was still gripping the kitchen counter with whitened knuckles.

"Then he—he went on the offensive. He said that he knew what happened between me and Gina, and how I..." Aaron cleared his throat. "How I didn't call her after. That things would look bad for me, if I treated girls this way. That he wouldn't want anything unsavory to get out in the press."

"He threatened you."

"I don't know. Maybe. It didn't matter—I knew he would never let his daughter get caught up in any sort of scandal. I told him that I had heard what had happened to a girl that had interviewed with him."

"He knew it was me."

"Yeah, he guessed. But I guarantee if we hadn't dated he wouldn't have known which person I was talking about. I'm sure you're not the first he's done this to."

Eliza only shrugged.

"I told him that if he ever tried to lay his hands on you again that we'd have a big problem. He asked if I was threatening him physically, and I said no, I was threatening to sue him. Or rather, fund a lawsuit involving every girl who had ever worked with him. I—I might have done a little research. Just on assistants that had come and gone, things like that. I mentioned a few names—I didn't know anything, just said them—and he got real quiet. He told me that he didn't think we would have any sort of problem like that, so long as I stayed away from his daughter. I told him that I'd come as close to his daughter as Gina wanted me to, and that no matter what, he'd never try to pull something like this again."

"Aaron," Eliza said, squeezing her eyes shut. "You know that's not going to help."

Aaron felt an arrow go through his heart. He was so powerless—he felt it all over again standing across from Eliza. He knew better than to expect praise, or gratitude, or even appreciation for his poor attempt at chivalry. But he wanted Eliza to understand. Understand how much he wanted to be there for her, to make up for times when he wasn't there to protect her or anyone else he cared about.

"Well, we came to some sort of understanding, at least. I left, and that was that. We didn't talk again."

"All you did was make sure that Lyle Tiller hated your guts. He's going to make your life a living hell until you quit or are cut or both."

"Doesn't matter. You know I'm not much longer for this career anyway."

"Good luck getting into business or anything sports-related after this."

"I'll manage. I have money. Hey, Becks was about to do it."

They both winced at the mention of their friend. "I should check on Whitney," Eliza said, slipping off of the stool. "She's had a rough day." She paused, staring at Aaron. "Look, I appreciate you trying. I really do. But I can handle myself. This is why I didn't tell you in the first place."

"I know."

"Men like Lyle Tiller are absolute vermin. You won't fix them, and you won't intimidate them into being better. The best we can do is just minimize contact. You promise me you won't try talking to him again?"

Aaron nodded, though he couldn't bring himself to verbally promise. If the man ever did try talking to Eliza again, threatening her...

"And you should have told me this earlier," Eliza said. "I wish you had."

"I wanted to, but I didn't want you to think that all of this had something to do with Gina's death," Aaron said. "I wouldn't be surprised if Lyle thinks I had a hand in it—he's not my biggest fan, after finding out."

"Who told him? About you and Gina."

"Gina, maybe. Who knows? Lyle said a few things to me about 'getting even' when I saw him, you know. It was creepy."

Eliza shuddered. "The best thing we can do is just never talk to him again," she said. "And for you to retire as soon as possible. What we were talking about earlier. I *can* make those connections for you. Connections far away from Lyle Tiller and his friends."

"I know, Lize. You're the best. Seriously."

Eliza walked over to Aaron and reached up to put her hands on his shoulders. "I love you," she said. "As a friend, of course. I love you, and I want what's best for you, and I will always be here for you."

"As a friend," Aaron repeated.

"Yes."

He grinned and opened his arms, and Eliza leaned in to give him a quick hug. "Maybe one day I'll be as good a friend to you as you are to me," he muttered, as they both pulled back.

Eliza snorted. "Good luck trying."

When she had left, Aaron sank down against his counters, breathing a deep sigh of relief. That done, he felt a thousand times lighter. Eliza knew all of his secrets now—and they were good. Better than good, really.

But he found, after the initial wash of relief, that something was still bothering him. The answer was obvious enough: Gina Tiller's death, and the cloud that was still hanging over them all as they waited for the police to figure out who did it. Aaron felt a strange sense of foreboding. He knew what people were whispering. He knew what the news articles would be saying before long, if they had been careful not to say it up until now.

He knew that things were not looking good for Daniel Becker.

CHAPTER 40

*B*ecks walked outside onto the deck, holding a steaming mug of coffee. He sat in one of the wicker chairs after tugging off the cover that Whitney had so neatly tied on for the winter. It had begun to snow, ever so lightly, and the sky was a dark and impenetrable mass hovering low over the town. He felt a strange sense of unreality, sitting there, as if he could reach up and cup the sky with his hand, as if he could lift himself higher and float towards the stars, away from all his problems. Away from himself.

His headaches were worse. They were sometimes blinding, preventing him from sleep. Though Becks supposed that was for the best, given his violent outburst against Whitney a few days ago.

He was having trouble speaking, too, which seemed to be a side effect of the pain. He would try to get a few words out and then his head would begin to pulse, and Whitney would look at him with that frightened expression on her face and ask if he needed something, a glass of water, an aspirin…? And he would grow short-tempered and say that *no*, for the millionth time, he was fine. Whitney would stiffen and tell him that he had to be careful of his tone, even if he was hurting, and Becks would feel rage bubble through him at the helpless-ness of his situation, at the fact that it was only getting worse, at his inability to control his pain or his emotions.

He wondered what would become of him. He would go to jail, certainly, or if not to jail then a mental hospital. He'd have doctors hovering over him all the time there, and just like the ones now, they would be careful and distant but curious, occasionally moving their gaze from his eyes up to his skull, as if they wanted nothing more than to split the bones open and see what the riddled insides looked like. Whitney would come to visit him sometimes, in a black dress and with no makeup, looking somber and sad and all the more beautiful. He would insist on a divorce, and she would protest, the always loyal Whitney, but then finally he would figure out a way—applying with the help, perhaps, of a sympathetic nurse—and finally free Whitney from the black vortex that had become his life.

When Becks replayed the past year, he still had trouble figuring out where it had all gone wrong. The tackle, certainly —but then, he hadn't been *trying* to hurt the guy. The only way he would have avoided the tackle and its aftermath was if he wasn't playing during those minutes, if he had been injured or otherwise indisposed, if his coach had moved him at the last moment, or the play had changed at the last second. But it hadn't, and Becks had moved inexorably towards his fate. He thought often of the man he had injured, thought often of sending something—flowers? A card? Money?—thought about how strange it was to suddenly be the object of some-one's intense hatred, and to be deserving of it, too. Becks had ruined one life, so he supposed it was fair that his own should be ruined, too. He could accept some karma in that.

If only he hadn't murdered Gina Tiller.

That's what bothered Becks the most about the headaches: they made it so hard for him to try to pull up any memories from that fateful night. Sometimes he swore he remembered seeing Gina in the bedroom, standing on the balcony, smiling over her shoulder at him. Other times the night was a complete black box. Becks had no idea whether his brain was supplying the memories, doing its best to offer him something to prove it wasn't the useless organ that it had, in actuality, become.

He could, however, easily pinpoint a motive for his rage. He only had to think back about Gina Tiller's little speech, her laughter, her mocking of the entire event and of Becks' staggered, hopeful emergence into Life After Football. She had insulted Evan. She had insulted Becks. Worst of all, she had insulted Whitney. And why? Because she was the spoiled daughter of a rotten, rich man, who thought it a spectacle to attend the fallen star's launch party and watch his world continue to burn. Becks shook when he thought of it. How careless her sadism was, how willing she was to wound just for a little bit of amusement. Never had Gina Tiller experienced anything like strife in her life, and so a woman like Gina Tiller could not even fathom what it was like to be on the receiving end of it. She would never know what it was like to watch your loved one, who had been through so much for you, be maligned in front of a crowd, all for a laugh. Becks squeezed his eyes shut.

In all, it would be better for Whitney, Becks thought. Better for him to go away, even if it *had* been an accident. He would be cut off from her life, allowing her to move on without him, without his cancerous being seeping into hers and destroying her life with his. It had been utter selfishness not to divorce her from the start. When he had come home that day, that awful day, and found Whitney waiting for him…. She had been so stoic, so calm. She had called his agent, his publicist, his banker. She had told him to rest, had reassured him that everything would be okay, even if he never played another day of football again. And of course, he hadn't.

Now Whitney had gone out again, on some trivial errand

that gave her an excuse to leave Becks. He knew she didn't need to go to the grocery store, or the post office, or the hardware store, half as often as she told him she did. He did know that she needed a break from Becks and his temper and his rotting mind, and needed that break more and more often recently. Becks thought about getting a beer from the fridge, only to be rebellious, only because he could—he hadn't touched alcohol since that day, afraid of becoming someone like Sam O'Nally (how cruel and fitting that Sam O'Nally was one of the two people willing to still show up to Becks' event!). But what did anything matter now? What was his life worth?

A knock came at the door.

Becks glanced lazily over. He wasn't in the mood for company, nor did he think he would be of any use to whatever friend, detective, or spectacle-seeker was there. But when the knock came again, loud and insistent, Becks sighed, head pounding, and walked over.

Rick Fales stood at the front door, smiling quickly and nervously as Becks opened it. "May I come in for a moment?" he said. "Your wife isn't home, I take it."

"She's out."

"Lovely. Can I come in?"

Becks wanted to form the word 'no,' but his head felt murky. Indeed, he was starting to feel a bit nauseous again. He moved aside and made for the bathroom; Rick followed him in and shut the door behind him.

When Becks emerged from the bathroom ten minutes later, Rick was sitting in the little-used dining room of the house. He had a glass of water before him, which he offered to Becks.

"No, thank you," Becks said. His head was still pounding, but he could at least see straight now, and he didn't feel like his insides were about to spill out of him.

"Drink it. It'll do you some good, maybe," Rick said. Becks weighed the options, decided it was less work to avoid the argument, and downed half the glass in one swig. He did, indeed, feel a little better. "Okay," Rick said. "I wanted to break it to you first."

"Break what?"

Rick looked uneasy. "I—I have to be honest. I was kind of hoping that Sam O'Nally had something to do with what happened to Gina. It just—it just kind of made sense, and then you don't seem like the type—"

"I don't want to talk about it."

"I know," Rick said, coloring. "I don't, either. But listen. You should know. Get yourself a good lawyer. Sam was caught on video when Gina fell. He didn't do it; he was outside. But he might've seen who did."

Becks' heart stuttered. "He saw me?"

Rick was studying Becks closely. "Possibly. If you were the one who pushed her."

"I don't remember."

"That's fine. That's all right. What I'm saying is, Sam saw something. So now you know—and I'd appreciate it if you didn't tell the detectives exactly where you found that out. But talk to a lawyer, figure out a strategy."

"A strategy."

"Yes. A defense strategy. You've talked to one already, haven't you?"

Had he? Becks' head was throbbing. He couldn't remember. There had been talk of it, certainly, perhaps a few phone calls, but he didn't think they'd gone to any offices to meet with someone, not yet. "I—I don't know."

"Well, I'd push Whitney to take you to someone. Right away. And when the police come, you don't talk to them, right?"

"Why are you saying this to me?"

Rick looked embarrassed. "I don't know. I don't think it's fair, somehow. You can barely defend yourself, so someone has to look out for you."

"Whitney is," Becks said automatically. And what wasn't fair was Gina Tiller dying. No matter how much Becks disliked her, he couldn't get around that. No insult was worth a murder. How could he ever atone for taking a life?

"Yeah, she is," Rick said. "But maybe she doesn't realize how serious this is. Maybe she still thinks...hopes that maybe you..."

"Didn't do it?" Becks said bitterly. "Yeah, I hoped that, too."

Rick was quiet for some minutes. "I'm sorry," he said finally. "I was really hoping it would end another way."

Through his fear and pain, Becks felt strangely touched. It had been a long time since anyone had seemed to believe in him like the little reporter, even if he ultimately hadn't deserved that belief.

"Thanks anyway," Becks managed.

"Don't worry about it. It's just—I can't believe it, really. That night. I wish it just made more sense."

"There's not much more to know," Becks said. But the reporter did not rise and leave, only sat there waiting. Becks felt another surge of rage—the man was curious, was he? Then let him understand just how depraved his pet ex-footballer was. "Maybe I sleepwalked—did Whitney tell you I do that sometimes? Used to freak my college roommates out. And I—I can get violent, I guess, when I do." He told Rick briefly about the most recent sleepwalking incident, watching for the horror and disgust on Rick's face as he told him about his wife's bruises. Rick only looked confused, and a little frightened.

"Sleepwalking," Rick repeated. "Is that a CTE thing?"

"Don't know."

"So you just went to take a nap that night? Right after Gina's speech? Was that it?"

Becks sighed. He didn't want to go over it again, when

they had discussed it so many times before. "Yes," he said. "I was feeling tired. So I just left."

"Did you tell anyone where you were going?"

"No. I went alone."

"Did anyone see you go?"

Becks racked his brain. "No. I don't think so. I was talking to Evan and Whitney right after the speech. Whitney wanted us to go. Evan said we had to talk to a few more people, or something. So we said a few more minutes."

"Who said a few more minutes?"

"Whitney. She agreed we'd stay a little longer."

"And you did?"

"Yes. Didn't I tell you this? I—I was starting to feel really sick. I looked over and I saw you talking—you were speaking to Sam. You guys were looking at me. I started to feel like everyone was talking about me and looking at me, and I just didn't want to be there anymore. So I took off. I think I said I was getting some water. Whitney saw me go, I guess," Becks finished, defeated. "I don't know. It's all muddled."

"Where did you go?"

Becks' voice grew quiet. "Towards the rooms. And then I woke up on the staircase. That's all I remember."

"Right," Rick said. His voice was strained, but he seemed to be trying to sound somewhat cheerful. "Well—that's. Nothing to glean from any of that. Could've been anything, really. An accident, like you said, or maybe...maybe..."

"Just stop," Becks said. "It doesn't matter. I don't want to know. It's over."

Rick grew quiet. They sat alone in the darkened dining room as the clock chimed 8:30. Becks breathed slowly, trying to let his mind float off, trying to disassociate himself from the world that had turned so cruel, from the dark person that he had somehow become.

"I'm going to turn myself in," Becks said, and he knew it

was bad when the journalist said nothing, only nodded slowly. There. The truth was in front of them, naked and ugly. But Becks would face it. Just like he had faced everything before. He had committed a crime, and he would take his punishment. There might not be fairness in the world, but there was justice.

"Wait," Rick said, as Becks moved to rise.

"I'll get an attorney," Becks said, a little annoyed. He didn't want to kill his momentum, knowing that his window of courage was small. If Whitney walked through the doors and begged him to stop, he knew he wouldn't be able to go through with it. "Eventually. I'll just—"

"No, wait!" Rick cried. "Wait." He leaped up and sprinted across to the kitchen. Becks followed him, confused. Rick gave a strangled gasp as he picked something up off the counter, and then began digging through the drawers.

"What are you doing?"

Rick froze in front of one of the cabinets, hand shaking. "Call the police, please," he said to Becks, in a strangely calm voice.

"I told you, I was going to turn myself in—"

The door to the house opened again, and a woman's voice floated into the kitchen. "Daniel? Daniel, who's inside?" Whitney walked into the kitchen, saw Rick, and froze. Becks looked from his wife to the journalist, not sure what to say, head spinning at the look of careful calculation suddenly passing between the two of them.

"I'm calling the police unless you get out right now," Whitney said.

"I'm calling them for you," Rick replied, and dialed.

CHAPTER 41

"Wait!" Whitney cried, pulling at Rick's arm. "Why? What are you doing?"

"Whitney?" Becks said, confused. Rick pulled his arm away from Whitney and came to a stop a few feet from her. When he looked up at Whitney, he knew that *she knew* that he knew. His heart picked up.

"Hold on," Whitney said, her voice lower, firmer. She didn't loosen her grip on Rick's arm, but he transferred the phone to his other hand and shrugged, swiping at the screen. "You don't need to call anyone. Just hold on a second."

"What's wrong, Whitney?" Becks said. The ex-footballer sounded both stern and confused. "Did something happen?"

"Let's talk, then," Rick said, and he saw the light leap in Whitney's eyes. He used her momentary distraction to take a step back and switch hands again. He waved her towards the couches. "After you."

"Come on, Daniel," Whitney said. "We're going to see what this gentleman wants before he leaves."

She sounded so calm, Rick thought. He typed quickly on his phone and pocketed it, so that when he came to sit across from Whitney and Becks, it was out of sight, no longer a

193

present, looming threat. He felt a rush of cold as he again came under Whitney's gaze.

"So," Whitney said. "You were going to call the police? Care to explain why?"

Rick spread his hands. "I was hoping you could clarify things a little for me, actually."

"I wasn't the one about to call the authorities."

Becks crossed his arms, looking troubled. Rick glanced at him and then away. It all just seemed so outlandish. But then, the bottle had confirmed it, hadn't it? The whole house of cards had fallen. If Rick was right...if his depraved mind had wandered to the correct dark places...

He had to show some cards, Rick thought. So Whitney knew he had something, without knowing all of it. If he didn't say anything, she would think she had misread him, that he was merely bluffing.

"Was it you or Evan who killed her?" Rick said.

Becks' eyes popped. He seemed to be about to rise from the couch when Whitney said, "Utter nonsense. Neither of us did anything to her."

"If you're not honest with me, I *will* call the police. And show them the pill bottle I found in the kitchen."

Whitney's eyes sparked. "Whitney," Becks said. "What's going on?"

"Nothing, Becks. Why don't you go take a nap? Mr. Fales and I have something to discuss. And I did tell you," she added viciously, "to not let him in the house anymore."

Becks blinked. Rick guessed he was trying to reconcile this hostile woman with his wife; Rick, with much less background on Whitney, was trying to do the same.

"Go," Whitney said. "Nap, Daniel. We'll talk when you're up."

He rose, teetering a little. But he walked only a few steps before he sank down into the armchair perpendicular to Rick.

"I want to stay," he said. And then, stronger, "I'm staying. I want to hear this."

"Daniel," Whitney hissed.

"No, go on," Rick said. "I think it's good for everyone. Get things out in the open. Start from the beginning, then. The night of the party."

"You think that's the beginning?" Whitney said, her steely eyes shifting back towards him. She glanced at her husband again, assessing. "Last chance," she warned.

And Becks did think about it. Rick saw him assessing, calculating. In his shoes, Rick didn't know what he would have done—the temptation would certainly have been high to disappear into some back room, to sleep while his head was throbbing, to wake up to the kinder wife that he knew, with his world still intact (or mostly intact).

But Becks just shrugged a little and said, "I'm staying."

Whitney shrugged back. "Fine. Your choice." Whitney checked her watch. "I have some time to tell you the story."

"Good. I have time to listen."

Whitney smiled at him. The expression held no warmth. "It wouldn't have gone down like this," she said, "if Daniel hadn't hurt that man."

CHAPTER 42

*W*hitney cleared her throat. She could feel both men watching her, waiting. Part of her derived a certain pleasure from their attention, from the knowledge that soon their minds would twist and expand with the truth, and they would see her as she really was, not as they always wanted and expected her to be. Daniel, poor, helpless Daniel, who trusted her so much, who wanted her to be everything for him even as he simultaneously acted noble and told her that she should never have married him. She shouldn't have, that was clear now, but what was done was done, and Whitney would make the best of it, as she always had.

And that journalist? He would see, too. He would see with an unsullied mind and a clear head, and he would understand —at least, understand what little he could before the end of the night. Before—well.

"It was my idea to start the company," Whitney said, directing her gaze at Rick. It was easier to tell him, somehow, to not look into Daniel's gaping eyes and tell him something he should have been able to guess months, if not years, before. "Once Daniel's football career was over, we needed a way to make income. It seemed like a good idea—especially since we had Evan, who was good with numbers, and who could help.

"Evan and I talked about ways to make sure that we had control of it, of course, in case things ever went south. That's where the contract came in—we would go into business together and invest the money, and that way it would be safe. It would grow over time, and Daniel, whatever happened to him, would benefit. He just wouldn't control it."

"So you made the contract of the company knowing that you'd cut Becks out of it," Rick said.

"Naturally," Whitney said. She still didn't look at Daniel. "It made the most sense. He wasn't in the right frame of mind to be able to contribute, you see."

"Sure. So far so good. So you decide to throw a party last weekend—"

"Evan's idea. I thought it was stupid. But he convinced me that we needed the marketing, that we had to start with a bang." Whitney rolled her eyes. "I suppose there's a joke in there somewhere. So I went along with it. Daniel was having a horrible time, of course."

"That was by design, wasn't it?"

"I don't know what you mean."

"You wanted people to see how sick Daniel was."

Whitney colored. It was closer to the truth than she would have liked. "I wanted to leave almost right away, actually. But Daniel said we had to stay, so we stayed." She drew in a long breath, as Rick and Daniel just watched her. *Anytime now would be good*, she thought, and shakily took another breath. Maybe this was as much of the truth as she wanted to tell.

"Gina," Rick pressed. "What happened with Gina?"

"Oh, she's a horrid woman. You heard that speech she gave in front of everyone. What did you think of that?"

"She sounded drunk."

"Of course. She always was." Whitney pursed her lips. "I didn't realize something was off about her that night until she stood up on that stage and said those horrible things about me. About Evan. It upset Daniel, too, that was obvious—at least she could have thought of that. But no. She had gotten it into her head that she was doing something righteous."

"Something righteous?"

It amazed Whitney how daft most men could be. "Yes. She decided that she didn't like the arrangement that Evan and I had set up. And she was going to have a talk with Daniel about it. You see, she overheard Evan and me talking earlier in the evening, and from whatever she pieced together, she decided that she had to be some avenging angel."

"How do you know that?"

"I'll get there. So after the speech, Evan comes down and we talk for a bit. I go to find Daniel and Evan goes to find Gina, to talk some sense into her. She had gone into one of the upstairs bedrooms. She knew he would follow her. She had told him earlier in the night—before that awful interruption— that she wanted Evan to tell Daniel what she had overheard, or else she would."

"So about the fact that you two planned to cut Daniel out of the company."

Whitney hesitated. She spared a quick glance at Daniel, who looked confused and hurt. She shifted her gaze back to Rick. "Yes. In any event, Evan knew what she wanted. And he knew that it was only a matter of time before she said something awful like that to Daniel, when really—why did he have to know? What good would it do him? So he walked into the room, and...well, I suppose they quarreled, and Gina fell over. And that was that."

"An accident?"

"How should I know?"

Rick frowned. "He confessed to you, obviously. If you're telling me about it."

She could see the fear slowly dawning on Rick's face. *Yes, you turtle-brain*, she thought. *I'm not telling you for my own conscience.* Aloud she said, "Yes, he told me what he had done. He didn't try to hide it. I assume it was some sort of awful accident—and there was no reason to ruin what was left of Daniel's future because of it."

"Or yours. Or Evan's."

Whitney shrugged.

"Did you go outside to check on Gina?"

"No, of course not. I didn't know what happened, not exactly. Evan just said it was something awful that happened on the balcony, and he had to tell me—I told him to be quiet for now."

"You're a pretty loyal business partner."

Whitney glared at Rick. *Rat,* she thought. "I'm a loyal person."

"Were you planning to tell Daniel that you were having an affair?"

Silence filled the room. Whitney felt like she was drowning in it. She didn't dare look at Daniel, though she could feel his eyes on her, could imagine the stiffened, shocked expression on his face, almost half-amused at the thought. She knew that if she looked at him, she might break down, might lose her resolve. *It wasn't supposed to happen like this,* Whitney thought.

"You really want him to know everything, then," Whitney said finally, lip curling in disgust. "You can't keep that out of it."

"He should know," Rick said. "Why shouldn't he?"

"Because he won't know for long."

Rick blanched. Whitney stared at him, hard. *He really could have left that detail out,* she thought, lips pursed together. *He really didn't need to say that.*

"Why won't he know long?" Rick said.

Whitney snorted.

"No, really. You're talking about CTE?"

"I'm not discussing it with you."

"Why not? If that's the case, why can't you say it?"

Whitney rolled her tongue behind her teeth. She had a number of choice words that she wanted to tell the journalist, but she bit her tongue. Some secrets were not meant to be told.

Rick whipped on Daniel. "You seemed to be a bit better, after the party. Fewer headaches. Wasn't that the case?"

"Whitney?" Daniel said. "What's going on? Are you—are you and Evan—?"

"They are," Rick said. Whitney still refused to look at Daniel. "Becks, this is important. The days after Gina died, you were feeling better, weren't you? When I came to visit, you seemed lucid. No headaches or anything, I think."

"I don't know. I felt a little better, I guess."

"Did you eat anything differently those days? Drink something, stop drinking something?"

"What? I don't know why you—I mean, nothing out of the ordinary. Except..." Daniel's voice trailed off, and he grew quiet.

Whitney couldn't bear it any longer. She looked up at him.

Daniel's eyes were searching hers. They didn't look angry, not yet, though that might come later—they looked incredibly sad. As though she had taken him and shattered him. As though he was still waiting for her to say the right words to explain it all away, to make everything better. That was Daniel's problem...he kept hoping and hoping, long after the situation was hopeless. She stared at him with her expression hard, unyielding, and slowly Daniel seemed to understand: there was nothing she could tell him to take it all away. Even lies at this point would be a bandaid on the wound, useless and temporary.

Daniel jerked his head left to face Rick.

"I was sick that morning," he said quietly. "The morning after. I threw up most of the day."

"And you felt better after that? Better than before, I mean?"

"Yes. I mean, not right away…but in the next few days, yes. I started to feel a lot better. A lot more clear-headed." His jaw worked. "I thought I was just getting more sleep, or something."

"And then it got worse."

Daniel pressed his palm to his forehead, as if acknowledging the source of the pain. "Yes."

"Care to explain?" Rick said to Whitney.

No, in fact. No, she did not. But she was terrified now, terrified that Rick would walk out too soon and leave someone wandering the world who knew things that nobody except Evan and herself ever should. "Fine," she said, discreetly checking her watch again. "We were dosing Daniel with medication."

"Medication? What kind?"

Whitney blew air through her nose. "Well, a home remedy, anyway."

"A poison."

"You can call it what you wish," Whitney spat. "It's all about dosages, anyway." At least, that was what she had told herself, when she first started giving Daniel the concoction— extract of Garcinia cambogia, high doses of Vitamin A, a rotating group of other herbs, and then (experimentally!) a little bit of arsenic. She herself had used an alternative medicine supplement back in the day that had trace levels of arsenic; the supplement had promised to help her sleep, and did. But Whitney had used a higher dosage for Becks. To make it more effective, she had told herself. To help his restless sleep, his headaches, his fatigue. She couldn't remember the moment she had switched over from trying to help Daniel to trying to poison him. In some ways, she felt like she never had. But she had understood that there were risks of giving him higher and higher dosages, that symptoms might mimic CTE, but then, it was entirely possible Daniel *did* have CTE, and the concoction was just helping him…

"When did you start? While Becks was still playing?"

Whitney felt a rush of rage. "Of course not. I would never. Only after he was finished. When we were home alone and I —I was helping him. He was depressed, and his head hurt, sometimes..."

"I told you it never did," Daniel said. Whitney kept her eyes on Rick. "I told you I would tell you if that started, and it didn't, not for a while. But you kept asking me if I had a headache, like you expected it. You brought up CTE two weeks after I left the NFL."

"Someone had to discuss the possibility."

"You said that I wasn't fit to work anymore. To go to business school. That I should let Evan start a company and be a figurehead, so that I could do something without exerting myself, you said. You told me there weren't any other options."

"I wasn't lying," Whitney said. "Why would you go to business school? It's a waste of money, and you'd never make it in a traditional corporate job. You've been an athlete your entire life, for goodness sake. You never worked an office job in your life."

"I had the money to waste if I wanted to."

"Yes, well, it's *my* money too. I gave up my career to support you, to keep our household together. I had a say in how we invested it."

"So you invested it in Evan. And not in me."

Whitney wheeled her gaze finally on her husband. "I was doing what I needed to do to keep things together," she said. "I'm sorry if you don't see it that way. After you were kicked out of the league...it was like the world was crumbling down on us. We have savings, Daniel, but I don't think you understand how much money it takes each year to keep this house. Not to mention the investment properties in Florida...we needed to do something. I reached out to Evan for help."

"Is that when it started?" Rick said. "Or...no, it was before, wasn't it?"

"What does it matter?" Whitney said, flushing. It hadn't been like that, not like Rick was implying. She and Evan had spent a night together once, years back...it had been silly then, just a simple transgression, one they agreed to never speak about so as to protect Daniel. And then when Daniel was fired, Evan was the only person that she could think to reach out to. The football players wanted to have nothing to do with him, of course. And Evan, Evan was Daniel's good friend from high school. And he had a reason to want to keep Whitney happy, too...

She had reached out, and Evan had come over that one evening to support them. He had cheered Daniel considerably. Whitney had walked him out to his car to thank him, and he had reached for her arm, and—they had been embarrassed after they had kissed, but they both knew it would go further next time. Wasn't it Evan, anyway, who had suggested increasing the dose of the herb? Whitney couldn't remember...if it was her, well, then Evan certainly knew about it and encouraged it. It was Evan who had told Whitney to have Daniel throw up the next day, in case the police wanted to drug test him and found strange levels of it in his system. They had kept him off of the herb for days after, until it became clear that they needed to do something, to risk it again, lest Daniel become more clearheaded and remember that, in fact, he had had nothing to do with Gina's death. That Evan and Whitney had been acting strangely...

They weren't trying to frame him, of course. That wasn't the intention, when Evan had killed Gina. It just so happened that afterwards, they saw it was a perfect solution. Daniel would be deemed crazy and would go to live in a mental ward. He would be safe there at least, drugged up and carefully monitored. Whitney knew something about such places. Even if you *were* sane, you wouldn't get out of one. That wasn't how they worked. Daniel would get the care he needed (after all, didn't most football players get CTE, at least eventually?) and Whitney and Evan could look after the money. If, in a few years, they decided to marry, well, that would be that. Whitney didn't care so much about the legal side of things.

"My sleepwalking," Daniel said, breaking Whitney's thoughts. "You said I had choked you."

Whitney stole the briefest glance at him. "Well," she said. "You *do* sleepwalk, of course."

"Did I touch you?"

Whitney's hand trailed across her neck. "No. You didn't."

"Who made the bruises?"

"Well, I did. But you have to understand, Daniel, I wanted you to take your health seriously." She colored at the expression on Rick's face. Who needed the beady-eyed little journalist there to judge her? He didn't understand. "Maybe it wasn't the best idea. But I wasn't trying to——"

"You wanted to make him think he was going crazy," Rick said incredulously. "You made him think that *he tried to kill you?*"

"Daniel, I knew that if you went to——to a facility——then you'd get all the care you needed."

"The DNA," Rick said. "You put Becks' DNA under Gina's fingernails."

Whitney snorted. "That was Evan's idea. He said juries love DNA evidence. It was just a piece of hair, anyway. He was going to do it in front of the security cameras, until I reminded him they were there."

Rick was looking at her as though she were a monster. *You don't understand*, she wanted to say. *You've never been married to a footballer.*

"You framed your husband for murder," Rick said.

Well, of course it would sound bad when he said it like *that...*

"I didn't kill anyone," Whitney said.

"But you knew that Evan was going to. You could have stopped him."

She was tired of this game. Of course she wasn't going to be able to explain it all to Rick in the short time they had. Of course she couldn't go into her deep history with Daniel, how she had stood by him when his family had not, how she had sacrificed, how she had done everything for him, how she had felt so betrayed the moment he had tossed it all away with that stupid tackle and then had come home and looked at her with tears in his eyes, as if he expected *her* to clean up the mess! After everything she had done for him, he still wanted more. Whitney was tired of it. And she had figured out a way to keep them both safe and happy, and shouldn't that have been enough?

"Whitney," Daniel said, voice pleading. "*Why?*"

"It was best for everyone, Daniel."

"But—"

The door to the back of the house opened.

CHAPTER 43

*R*ick almost jumped out of his chair. *Not yet,* he thought. *Just a few minutes longer…*

But he froze as Evan Miller, in a button-down shirt and business pants, walked into the room as if he were strolling home after a day of meetings. He looked fresh-faced and young in the low lamps of the Becker house, his cheeks just a little flushed, his eyes bright and searching.

"Whitney?" Evan said. "What's going on?"

Rick looked between the two co-conspirators, feeling tense. He worried about Becks, mostly, who had shifted in his seat to stare at his former best friend. What if the two men began fighting?

"Evan," Whitney said coolly. She had not lost her composure this entire time, not shed a tear or even spared more than a few glances at her husband. Rick felt cold every time he looked at her. "We were just chatting. Care to sit down?"

"Is Becks okay?" Evan said, wheeling towards his friend. Becks looked white, almost frail.

"Whitney was just telling us about how you were framing Becks for Gina's murder," Rick said, taking a risk. *Keep the conversation going,* he thought to himself. *At least until…*

"We were *what*?" Evan said, his gaze darting to Whitney.

"Framing Becks for Gina's murder," Rick repeated calmly. Next to him, Becks stirred.

Evan spared one scathing look at Rick before turning back. "Whitney, *what is going on*?"

"I was just talking," Whitney said calmly.

"You're trying to say this was on *me*?" Evan said, taking a few steps towards them, looking almost pleading as he came parallel to where Rick was seated, shoulders squared towards Whitney. "That *I* killed Gina?"

Rick felt a *whoosh* of cold go through him. Next to him, Becks seemed disoriented and out of it, and Rick couldn't tell if that was just the shock to his system, or if his symptoms were flaring up again. Had Whitney dosed him today?

"Evan," Whitney said, voice still calm, though with an electric note through it. "Please. We were just talking about a few things. I didn't see—"

Rick felt a tremendous pressure around his neck.

For a moment, nothing made sense. He flapped and flailed, and his first thought was *my goodness, I've caught my sweater on something.* But that thought was gone in a flash, replaced as soon as his mind processed that it was an arm around his throat, and that Rick had been so busy worrying about Becks that he hadn't noticed Evan turning around and attacking him.

They were bluffing, he thought stupidly. *They were pretending to argue so that they could take care of me.*

And then it was hard to think, because his vision began to swim and stars dotted his eyes. He tried to fight, swinging his arms up and kicking his legs. But he had been taken by surprise; he had let his guard down among murderers, and was paying the price.

His last coherent thought was that he felt sorry for Becks —that no one deserved what had happened to him, and that now no one would be around to tell his side clearly. Who knew if the effects of the poison were permanent. Who knew what would become of him. Poor, poor Becks…

The world went black.

Rick crumpled to the floor. He inhaled deeply, gasping, his throat throbbing. He just had time to process Becks' feet in front of him before he heard a tremendous *crash* and the sound of shattering glass.

Trembling, Rick pulled himself to a sitting position. *I'm not dead*, he thought dumbly, massaging his throat as he looked towards the sound of the crash. Evan lay slumped amidst broken glass, bleeding and groaning, but not severely hurt—at least, Rick didn't think so. Becks stood facing him, hands balled into fists, face a mask of rage.

Whitney had risen, her face white, her eyes calculating. "Becks," Rick tried to say, but his throat was hoarse. *Watch her. She'll try next.*

"Police! Hands up!"

Rick almost crumpled with relief. What had taken them so long? He had texted them as soon as Whitney had come home and told them that Whitney was confessing her crime to him. She had, eventually—just as Rick had hoped. The detective Rick had contacted must have told everyone to hold off until the sound of the crash.

"I want a lawyer," Whitney said, standing tall.

"You'll get one," one of the detectives replied, strolling up to her. "Hands behind your back, please."

"Hospital," Rick managed to choke out, motioning to one of the detectives. He pointed at Becks.

"Yes, we'll get you to the hospital, Mr. Fales."

"With Becks. He comes, too."

The detective looked at the tall ex-footballer, who now seemed lost, looking around the living room that was being infiltrated with cold night air, covered in shattered glass, and swarming with detectives, all as his best friend was tended to by an EMT and his wife was led out in handcuffs. "You, Mr.

Becker," the detective said. "You come with Mr. Fales, okay?"

"We'll ride together," Rick said. Except his throat was still raw, and it came out more as *wi-righ-tether.*

Becks stared at him, eyes wide and unfocused. Finally, he nodded.

CHAPTER 44

he headlines followed rapidly. *Football star's wife tries to frame him for murder*, and *Athlete's wife and best friend commit murder to cover up their affair*, and *Is this the real reason Daniel Becker went crazy?*

Rick contributed to none of them. He never sent the article to his editor and was prepared to spend a month in his van in consequence. Except, when he told his landlord he would be late that month, the usually surly man had declared that this was "Absolutely understandable!" and asked if, in the meantime, Rick wouldn't mind taking a picture with him?

For somehow, by stepping out of the story as a writer, Rick had stepped into it as a character. So many of the news articles mentioned that a "friend" and "well-known journalist" had helped piece together the case. No doubt some of this was self-absorption on the part of these journalists, believing that only a fellow writer would have the skills and tenacity to solve such a complicated crime. And no doubt the rest of it was pure storytelling: it was more exciting that, in the end, Rick had almost been murdered, and Becks had saved his life.

The police, it turned out, had already known that the DNA under Gina's fingernails was a plant: it was too perfect, a single hair of Becks', without any skin cells. They had been trying to ferret out who had framed him—Rick's risk that night had only sped up their conclusions.

Evan and Whitney opted to be tried separately. Whitney threw Evan under the bus: her lawyer claimed that Whitney had no idea that he had murdered Gina, and that she had *not* been poisoning Becks, but only practicing some alternative medicine. Evan, for his part, claimed that it all had been Whitney's idea, and that he had only been the muscle behind her schemes. Rick believed neither of them, though he sometimes worried whether Whitney's account would be more believable, if Whitney would play the grieving, beautiful, loyal wife well enough to garner sympathy.

At least, Rick would think then, *the police have my recordings.*

As for Rick, he was ready to move on from the circus that followed. He had to lay low for the weeks after, but it gave him time to plot out his next move. For he was certain of one thing in particular: he did not want to go back to reporting. It was time for a change, and he had an idea in mind of what that change could be.

Rick felt a flutter of nerves at the thought. But if the past few weeks had taught him anything, it was to follow his gut.

And also maybe to have a six-eight footballer around for backup. Just in case.

CHAPTER 45

S am O'Nally had mixed thoughts about the arrest of Whitney Becker and Evan Miller.

On the one hand, he felt a bit pleased that they hadn't gotten away with anything, after all. He was sick of their smug faces, acting better than him and refusing to help him, as though *he* were the bad guy. Disgusting hypocrites, that's what they all were.

On the other hand, he was disappointed it meant that the secret was out, that Sam would, in fact, get nothing from Evan to keep him quiet about what he saw that night. And oh, how Sam had tried to make a little something from it! He had gone to Evan and Whitney, of course, but also to Eliza, thinking that perhaps Eliza would want to protect her best friend. In a moment of desperation he had even tried Aaron, thinking Aaron wouldn't want Becks involved, even tangentially...but of course none of it had worked out. No money for him, because Evan and Whitney couldn't keep their mouths shut, and because they hadn't had the sense to pay him from the start.

And Sam *had* been surprised that night. He didn't like Gina himself, no one did, but what a shock it was to see the woman being pushed from the window! Sometimes, Sam still had nightmares about the *crack* that her head had made against the pavement. It was Evan who had leaned out, who had peered down with hard, beady eyes to see if she was dead. Evan who had come out to the deck (as Sam hid nearby) and slipped something under the woman's fingers.

And then he had seen Evan talking to Whitney later, right before the police arrived. He had watched as Evan held onto her arms and she pressed his hands. They had spooked when Becks had joined them, though Sam didn't think anyone else had noticed but him. *Interesting,* Sam had thought. *Very interesting.*

The police had been relentless in their questioning. "Why didn't you bring this up before?" they all wanted to know.

"Well, I must have forgot."

They weren't satisfied with this, of course. A few of them even guessed that Sam had been trying to get something out of Whitney and Evan in exchange for his silence. But when they threw such accusations at him, he only sat back and smiled. They couldn't pin it on him—that was the long and the short of it.

"You could have helped out your friend Becks," one of the detectives said during one such long bout of questioning. "If you knew his wife and his best friend were conspiring to frame him. You didn't think about that?"

"I didn't know they were framing him." Sam shrugged. "I feel sorry for the guy, but it's not my problem. I have enough of my own."

He hadn't liked the expression on the detective's face after that, and had scowled and asked to go. He gave a formal state-ment to the detectives about what he saw, and after a long talk with one of them, where charges were mentioned offhandedly and different "options" discussed, agreed to go to a rehab facility two hours upstate.

"I think you're making the right decision," the detective had said solemnly.

Sam had snorted. "We'll see."

At least, Sam thought, Becks had an end to his nightmare. Sam wasn't sure he would ever wake up from his.

ecks used a shoehorn to shove his feet into the black loafers that Eliza had picked out for him for this day. They were shiny, almost embarrassingly so, and Becks felt like the novice football player who went on the field with brand-new, unbroken-in cleats. But when he caught a glimpse of himself in the mirror, he stood a little taller. This was a different Becks. A new Becks.

His headaches were almost gone now, one year later. Occasionally he would still have one, or wake up in a hot sweat, but his doctor told him that this was likely psychosomatic. "So, made up," Becks would say, and his doctor would shake her head vigorously and go into a long explanation of the "great power of the brain."

The divorce papers had come in one week before, a rather pleasant surprise before his first day. Becks had been warned that such things could take a long while, especially given that his estranged wife was in jail. But Whitney, perhaps on the advice of her attorney, had signed in exchange for a small lump sum—maybe something, Becks thought, that would help her start over after the fifteen-year sentence was served.

Most days, when he let himself think of what had

happened, he hated Evan more than Whitney. Which was unfair—he knew how smart Whitney was, knew that she was likely the mastermind behind the scheme (no matter what she had said in court), knew that it was Whitney who had poisoned him, and Whitney who had originally figured out how she could part Becks from most of his money—and likely leave him for his best friend. But to Whitney he could only muster a cold indifference now; she had been his closest confidante and greatest support for so many years, and then he had discovered that what he thought of Whitney was but a strained veneer. He didn't know the woman beneath: he could pity her, and that was it.

But Evan? Evan had wept in front of Becks in court. He had begged for forgiveness. He had said that he didn't know why he had done what he had done, that he was sorry, that he deserved to go to jail. And Becks hated him. He hated the friend who had so willingly betrayed him for money, for Whitney, for a chance to usurp part of Becks' life. All the more so because Evan had once been someone Becks could rely on. He could not even trust the remorse, though he wanted to. He thought that if Evan could erase it all and go back to the night of the party, Evan would do everything exactly the same way (except, maybe, be a little more tight-lipped around Gina Tiller).

Becks swept the thoughts away. *Onward and up.* That was what the therapist had said to him, in one of the few sessions he promised Eliza he would attend.

"Looking sharp," Aaron said, emerging from the condo's living room and clapping Becks on the shoulder. "You look like you could fit in with those business school dweebs now."

"That's the plan," Becks said, grinning.

"Eliza is coming over with wine tonight. You good with red? We're going to celebrate."

"Whatever's fine. What can I pick up?"

"Nah, this is on us. We have to celebrate your big day."

Becks snorted. "Let's wait until I graduate, maybe, to get excited."

"Uh-huh, sure," Aaron said. "Tonight, seven sharp! Unless you're getting drinks with your business school buddies—then we'll have a rain check. Networking is ninety-nine percent of it, am I right?"

Becks smiled.

The nerves hit him again as he was walking to his car. Becks had applied to the nearby business school on a whim—it had a top-notch reputation, was in the city, and was exactly what he had wanted to do before Whitney had talked him out of it. He had done it as a sort of personal rebellion and never believed he would get in, not until he held the acceptance letter in his hand. He had tested all right, after the poison had worn off, his recommendations were solid, and his interviews had gone surprising well, but even then...part of Becks still expected everyone and everything to reject him at some point.

A fresh start, though. That was what it promised. He shivered a little as he climbed into his car, rubbing at a nonexistent spot on his chin. On the whole, the past year had been one of great fortune, though it was hard to appreciate it all, coming off of the events of the past spring. He had moved into Aaron's place last summer, in what was supposed to be a temporary situation as Becks sold his house, until both of them found that they liked the company more than their independence. And Becks tried to be of some help to Aaron, too, now that Aaron was retired and moving on to his own sales job in the city.

Eliza had been another pleasant surprise. At first, Becks hadn't known how to treat her: she had been Whitney's friend, after all, and Becks had always had a cordial but respectfully distant relationship with her. But Eliza had supported him immediately; she had visited Whitney in jail, "to see if she expressed remorse," Becks heard her tell Aaron later, but beyond that was supportive and even forceful in setting up

Becks' doctors' appointments, and checking in with him about his business school application deadlines and required court dates. The three of them—Eliza, Aaron, and Becks—made a strange sort of family, eating dinner together two or three nights a week, carefully avoiding talk about the past as they settled into their new routine. Becks was sometimes surprised that Eliza and Aaron were not together, but he never commented on it, lest he say something too caustic or cynical about love.

Becks had gone on dates over the past year, of course—often instigated by Eliza. She had set him up on two blind dates, and one of them had become a two-month long fling, a woman who was sweet and bubbly but who seemed to Becks to be more interested in him as an ex-footballer than as a man. Becks had been relieved when it had ended: mostly he had wanted to prove to himself that he could still get back out there, whatever "out there" meant.

His thoughts drifted as he drove towards the business school campus for his orientation. In some ways, Becks still felt fractured beyond repair. He had seen a brief surge in sympathy after the arrest of Whitney and Evan, because the press seemed to love a sad sap story. Some had even suggested that Whitney had poisoned Becks during his football career, blaming her for the tackle. Becks had been the recipient of dozens of fan letters from women who told him that they "knew for a fact" that it had all been Whitney's fault and that they would show him how a man should be treated, et cetera et cetera. Becks had felt sick to his stomach.

But when the news cycle had ended, and when Whitney and Evan were finally sentenced, everything died down once more. Becks became just another ex-footballer who was no longer welcomed in the NFL's circles. The only person who still spoke to him was Aaron, and whichever of Aaron's friends deigned to talk to him when they saw him. Nothing had changed, except Becks was stripped of the life he had had before: of a wife and a best friend and a future that had been perhaps not what he had envisioned, but had promised something of happiness.

Now, what did he have? A new future, a new promise, but mostly a blank slate. It could hold happiness, or it could hold heartache and betrayal. Becks no longer had faith that everything would work out for the best, not when life had taught him otherwise.

The silver lining, the only positive, had been the realization that he did not have CTE—at least, not yet. His symptoms cleared in the weeks and months after Whitney went to jail, and the numerous doctors who examined him assured him that he was as healthy as any other 29-year-old man. Becks no longer woke up with the looming fear that his mind was betraying him and that he might one day hurt the people he loved. He no longer felt the window of his future closing in on him, promising madness, hallucinations, and destruction.

Becks felt his stomach flip over as he pulled off the exit to the campus. The problem with blank slates was that they were blank—empty and foreboding. Part of him still worried that he would spend one week in classes and realize he didn't belong, that the other students would stare at him wide-eyed and refuse to work with him, or be kind to his face and cruel behind his back.

Becks could no longer stomach anyone who was even a little two-faced.

He parked and checked his phone. Rick had texted him with a picture of Becks' puppy (a rescued German Shepherd mix, adopted at Eliza's encouragement). *I'll bring him back tonight? Aaron said we're doing drinks.*

Yes, please, Becks said. *Thanks for watching him.*

Rick had been a surprise. The weaselly reporter who first seemed to want to write a story on Becks' insanity had turned out to be the one who had saved him. Becks had been far from grateful at the start—in fact, he had resented the man who had torn down the façade of his life. But they had seen each other in court a few times afterwards, and Rick had mentioned that he was finished with journalism and looking at other jobs.

It was loneliness or desperation that caused Becks to blurt out, "I need some help, actually. Temporary. It's simple work." He had blushed and explained that he wanted someone who could oversee the breakdown of his old house, who could sort through Whitney's things and his clothes and their furniture, saving the bare minimum and disposing of the rest.

Becks had been embarrassed almost instantly that he had asked, but Rick was interested, and not overly so. They had been tentative with each other at first, texting only, all business, Becks wiring the money over to Rick at the end of each week. After a month, Rick was offered a teaching job at the university, no doubt in part due to the fame of the recent case. *Journalism for dummies*, Rick had said. *Guess we'll be neighbors, once you get in.* The jobs between them ended, but they stayed in touch. Eventually, Becks worked up the nerve to tell Eliza to invite Rick over. He had been worried his friends would see his friendship with Rick as some sort of weird fixation on what had happened months before—but if they thought so, they never said, and Rick became a regular fixture at the apartment. It turned out the journalist was funny, when he wanted to be, and never sycophantic (though he, like so many others before him, had to get over an early crush on Eliza before he became really comfortable).

Becks placed his phone back in his pocket and let his hands rest on the steering wheel. Then, wrenching himself out of the seat, he climbed into the warm fall light.

He felt self-conscious as he joined the streams of students walking towards the auditorium. Fall had come early that year; whirls of red and brown leaves peppered the paved walkways that snaked across the green quads. Becks' eyes rested briefly on a statue of a man on horseback wielding a spear, and then on the wide steps leading up to the campus library.

He could feel eyes on him as he walked and told himself it was just because of his height, and not because anyone recognized him. He was much skinnier than in his football days, and his hair had grown darker, less sun-kissed. He had shaved his beard, too, and nowadays it was rare for him to hear the curious "Daniel Becker?" of a passing stranger.

He loped into the auditorium, double-checking the map in his orientation packet. He felt a few people smile at him as they walked in, the bland, friendly smiles of people who are beginning something new and looking to make friends. Becks tried to muster a smile back. His jaw felt tight.

He sat near the back—old habits, he never liked anyone being behind him—and folded himself down into one of the chairs near the aisle so that he could stick his legs out the side. The auditorium filled up quickly as the minutes counted down, and Becks could see the administrators fussing with the podium on the stage. He tapped his foot on the side of the stairwell, and with an effort stilled it.

"This seat taken?" a boy asked. For he *was* a boy, no older than twenty-three or twenty-four, perhaps, with a bright, beaming face and a mop of dark hair. Becks grunted and stood to make room for the boy to pass.

"Andrew Chung," the boy said, reaching out his hand. "Dang, it's a big class, isn't it?"

"It is," Becks said, clasping the boy's hand in his. "You local?"

"No—I'm from Connecticut, actually. You? And I didn't catch your name."

Becks blushed. Now or never. "Daniel," he said. And then, with an effort, "Daniel Becker."

Bless him—the boy's face remained bland and bright. "Great to meet you, Daniel!" he said. "I'm trying to remember names—my dad said that's what you have to do, right from the start. Nobody likes any word as much as the sound of their own name."

"I'll keep that in mind," Becks said with a quick smile.

The auditorium continued to fill; Andrew continued to chatter endlessly about college, and his consulting gig right after college, and how he planned to go back to said consulting gig, "considering they're paying for all this—ha! What did you do?" Becks was saved from answering as finally, at a quarter past nine, the lights dimmed, and the crowd grew quiet. A professor took the stage, launching into a welcome speech, encouraging them all to "get to know one another" and to "look around—for your future is around you in the connections you form here."

Becks half-listened. He couldn't still his nerves. But he was certain of one fact, as the professor continued—his future was indeed here, and he would make sure it was vastly different than his past.

ACKNOWLEDGMENTS

I'm so appreciative to have worked with so many wonderful and talented people on this title.

Thank you as always to Caroline and Alexandra for their their beautiful cover design and sharp edits, respectively.

A huge thank you to Joyce and Lesley, for their great feedback.

To my family, I love you so much. I wouldn't want to walk through this world with anyone else.

Finally, reader, thank you. I'm so grateful that you decided to spend some time in St. Clair.

ALSO BY L. C. WARMAN

To get exclusive content and stay up-to-date on L.C. Warman's new releases, subscribe to Greenleaf & Plympton's newsletter by visiting our website (https://www.greenleafandplympton.com).

ST. CLAIR MYSTERIES:

The Disappearance of Charlotte Walters

The Last Real Girl (Book 1)

The Last Real Crime (Book 2)

The Last Real Secret (Book 3)

The Eastwick Mansion Mysteries

A Death at Eastwick (Book 1)

A Scandal at Eastwick (Book 2)

A Betrayal at Eastwick (Book 3)

ABOUT THE AUTHOR

L.C. Warman is the author of the St. Clair mystery series. She grew up in New England, in a town where real estate contracts stipulated that you couldn't back out if you discovered your new place was haunted. She currently lives in a Michigan lakeside town with her husband and two dogs.

CPSIA information can be obtained
at www.ICGtesting.com
Printed in the USA
LVHW051004020320
648681LV00001B/90